Heart

of a

Lion

OTHER BOOKS BY EMORY R. FRIE

Heart of a Lion

THE REALMS SERIES:
Wonderland
Neverland
Enchanted Forest
Giant Country
Realm of the Snow Queen (Coming Soon!)

Heart of a Lion

By Emory R. Frie

Heart of a Lion by Emory R. Frie

First published in 2016
This edition published in 2019

ISBN 978-0-9974354-5-0 (Paperback)

This is a work of fiction. Names, characters, places, and incidents either are the products of the author's imagination or are used fictitiously. Any resemblance to actual persons, living or dead, businesses, companies, events, or locales is entirely coincidental. Use of any copyrighted, trademarked, or brand names in this work does not imply endorsement of that brand.

Cover Design: Emory R. Frie
Cover Images © Shutterstock

www.emoryrfrie.weebly.com

This book is dedicated to my amazing parents, who have been with me every step of the way;
And to my Lord, Jesus Christ, without whom none of this would be possible.

$\mathcal{P}$rologue

What was that? Spinning around, I saw a shrieking woman with a crying baby in her arms, a furious lord raising his whip for the snap. I ran. I didn't know quite why I ran; maybe it was a force of nature, but how could I let a young mother and infant be trampled by a raging horse and have a whip crack on their backs? I couldn't let that happen!

Shoving the woman out of the way, I shouted a single, yet sharp word to her: "Run!"

A slash ripped across my back like a burst of fire. Biting my lip to keep from screaming out, I fell on the ground from the impact. Rolling out of the way, the horse's hooves missed me as they thrashed the ground next to my head. The lord's curses bellowed at me as I scrambled to my feet. Throwing his fist in the air, he attempted to lay another burst of flames upon my spine, but this time the whip missed its mark and I ran with as much speed as possible after the woman who appeared to be slowing down from the weight of her baby.

My back screamed in pain! It must've been bleeding, but I had to get the two to safety. After all, one lash wasn't going to kill me. Quickly catching up with the crying woman, I snatched the babe from her, cradling him in one arm while grabbing the lady's hand with the other.

Harsh voices and trampling hooves signified that our pursuers were catching up. We turned into a dark alley and hid behind a stack of boxes and crates, trying to hush the crying babe. When the guards rode past, I let out a breath of exasperation. The woman looked at me, obviously surprised that a twelve-year-old girl just saved her life. Sitting in the silence, my back filled the gap with stinging pain. We both gasped for breath as I handed her back the whining child.

"Thank you for saving us," she whispered.

"You're welcome," I replied as I checked to see if the guards had come back for us. They hadn't.

"What is your name?" she asked.

I was bleeding, out of breath, and she wanted to know what my name was? I didn't mean to be rude or anything, but what would've really been useful right then would be if she had some medical experience or at least bandages.

"Sam," I simply said instead of the other remarks I really, I mean *really* wanted to say.

"I'm Elizabeth and this is Owen." She hugged her baby tighter, rocking him back and forth to calm him.

"Do you know where you live from here?"

"Yes."

"Then you should probably get there as soon as possible before the guards come back."

She smiled slightly. "I hope we meet again."

"I doubt that will happen," I muttered under my breath as she ran off. My eyes followed Elizabeth until she turned around the corner and vanished.

Deciding the coast was clear, I strolled out the way we came in, but as I turned the corner I quickened my pace… big mistake! A huge man, one I swiftly recognized as a guard, shouted something I didn't understand. The next thing I knew, fifteen guards surrounded me and in the middle of it all was the angry lord, his face red as a cherry and his belly round as a pumpkin. Well, maybe a bit bigger than a pumpkin.

Lord Cherry Face, for that's what I decided to call him, was huffing and puffing with anger and exasperation. He pointed his sausage finger at me and said between breaths, "She's... the... one. Give... me... the... whip!"

One guard handed Cherry Face the meanest looking whip I'd ever seen! I covered my head and turned away, trying to dodge the blows sure to happen. Fire jolted down my back with a force I never thought possible to give. The pain was like nothing I'd ever felt. I tried to escape only to be grabbed by two guards and have another flame catch on my back. The pain far too much for me, my knees gave way from beneath me and I collapsed. Though nothing made contact, my back seemed to repeat every lash with the throb of each wound. As the darkness began to close in from my shock, I didn't think I could take another strike.

"Stop!"

The voice belonged to a stranger, one not a part of Lord Cherry Face's group. Whoever he was, he seemed to have forced a stop to the whipping. Thank goodness. I struggled to stand, my knees still shaking and my back burning. Despite my attempts to keep them back, tears rolled down my face. Blood seeped through my shirt. It would most likely remain bloodstained until I found a replacement in the garbage.

Hesitantly, I looked up to see a man, an important looking man on an important looking horse. As more tears fell, I noticed a crown sitting atop his head. *King Richard.* Quickly brushing them back, I inclined my head, the pain in my back sure to explode if I bowed any more than that, but I kept my eyes on him. I studied his features. His brown beard was neatly trimmed, his clothes elegant, but what my gaze kept falling on was his eyes.

I hadn't seen eyes look at me so tenderly and lovingly in a long time. When people actually did look at me, all I saw was scorn or occasionally sympathy. The privileged mostly didn't look at me at all so they could pretend there was nothing else important in the world outside their own little lives. The King's eyes spoke something different. They showed love—a love that I'd only seen a long time ago, or looked upon others, but hardly ever on me. I never wanted him to stop looking at me like that.

"What is your name, child?" he asked in such a tender tone.

"Sam," my voice was nothing more than a squeak. I cleared my throat. "Sam."

"Ah, Samantha. I saw what you did to protect that woman."

"Yes, um, sire, I, uh…" I stammered.

"I congratulate you! It takes great courage to give your back to save another. You will be rewarded greatly."

The shock took me aback. "Um… that's not necessary, sire."

"Your parents should be very proud to have a daughter with such a brave and humble heart."

My face grew hot. "I honestly wish I knew if they would be, sire."

"Hmm," he pondered something. What? How he was to punish me? How he was going to make my life even more miserable than it already was? No, his eyes spoke differently.

"Samantha, do you have any family?" he questioned at last.

"No. Well, there was one… once," I said softly, "but not anymore." I looked down at my feet, trying to forget the question.

"I'm sorry to hear that." He scratched his chin and again I wondered what he was thinking. "Samantha," he said at last, "do you know my wife Veronica and I don't have any children?"

I really wished he would stop calling me *Samantha*. Wait! What did he ask me? "Yes?"

"Would you like to be our child?"

"Uh… is that a trick question?"

"No," King Richard chuckled—not an evil, mocking chuckle, but a kind and gentle one.

The question made me forget all about Lord Cherry Face, my bleeding back, and even Elizabeth and Owen. Have a family again, with the King? I hadn't had a family in four years. Now I had the chance to be in one again, a very slim chance, but a chance none the less. Was I about to pass up an offer like that?

But there was no way it could work! There had to be some catch, some unforeseen issue in becoming the adopted child of the King and Queen. And what about Queen Veronica? Who's to say she would want me? Would the people, the lords and ladies, the knights, even those who simply lived in the kingdom of Etheland, ever accept an

11

adopted princess? Would a street rat for an heir cause King Richard to lose respect?

Then again, the King would never ask me such a question if he didn't intend to solve all manners of legal and social matters. I could have a family again. Wasn't that what I long for most? Had God answered my prayers at last? I admitted that this wasn't at all what I expected or intended, but God seemed to be giving me an opportunity. How could I give up this miracle?

I put a smile on my face and answered, "Sire, I would love to be part of your family."

Chapter One

Sitting by the fireplace, I watched the flames dance. Even being Master of my household and leading knight of this territory, boredom still seeped into my mind. If only King Richard would hold a joust, I would instantly ride for the castle, sign up, and show all those other knights what William of the Silver Blade could do! The clanging of my armor, the cheering of the crowd, the sound of metal smashing metal, the sweat on my brow and the proud feeling of victory... A loud bang on the door interrupted my daydream.

"Come in," I shouted.

John, my squire and friend, swung open the door. He was a loyal boy, mature for his age. He helped me with my problems and actually listened to me when I wished for someone to speak honestly. Some people found it a bit odd that I was best friends with a fifteen-year-old and I was twenty-three. I didn't care, though. To me, friends had no boundaries.

"What is it, John?" I asked.

"Sir William," John stated, "the royal squire has arrived with an invitation from King Richard."

"John, how many times do I have to tell you to just call me Will?" I insisted.

"I apologize, Sir… I mean Will," he stammered.

I shook my head with a grin. "Now, what is this about an invitation?"

"His Majesty King Richard has arranged a joust and he would like you to take part in it."

It was as if John and King Richard had read my mind! "Well you go tell the squire that I would *love* to join the joust," I exclaimed excitedly while reaching for my sword, "and pack your things." I swung my sword around. "We're heading out in the morning."

My mother had given me one of her old rings when I was very young. I fingered it now in the habit I've developed over these many years whenever I wished to feel her presence and comfort. It hung on a chain around my neck so I could keep it with me at all times, a way to keep a little bit of her with me. It had two intertwining golden vines that wrapped around a small emerald in the front of the ring possessively. This ring was my most precious possession, even among all of the jewels and luxuries of which the Queen encouraged me to wear instead. I could never bring myself to bear such extravagant attire. It never felt right, and certainly not comfortable.

Queen Veronica never did approve of my modest choice of style, not to mention the horror she had upon my wearing men's clothes, and though she had tried her very hardest to make me into the proper young lady she declared all princesses—adopted or not—must be, it hadn't turned out the way in which she hoped. I learned skills from her, just not always put to the same use she expected. For instance, sewing skills were quite useful for mending a torn shirt and stitching up a split wound. And the art of dance could be useful in some instances of fighting, keeping in step with your partner and being prepared for the moves to change. The Queen and I did not always see eye to eye in such occasions or decisions, but she was a good mother to me even if she wasn't my true mother.

I looked out the window at my father's country, Etheland. I remembered that day nine years ago when King Richard took me in as his own. Even today, I couldn't see how he could adopt a street rat like me. Such kindness was something I could only try to live up to. Looking away, my gaze went to the crossed swords on the wall.

That day, that amazing day two years ago filled my mind. It was the day when I—as in *me*—was knighted at nineteen to become the only woman in Etheland to be a knight. I remembered all of the training I went through to get where I was now. It was near impossible to find someone to train and mentor me, but at last, King Richard found a knight and lord willing to give me a chance, though I was only a girl. Sir Hugh of the Iron Stone trained me well, as did the King when he had the time. I even got to the point where I could beat both men in any form of combat. Thus was when King Richard knighted me, taking the risk of exposing that a woman—his adopted daughter none the less—had been training in the way any normal squire would and more to be a knight. The matter went a lot better than most expected. I smiled at the happy memory.

Glancing at the fire leaping in the hearth, the horrible childhood memory of the day I became an orphan popped into my head. I was eight years old on the day I was carrying the buckets of water from the well to my house. Humming a song, I suddenly encountered my house, the place I called home, aflame. I dropped the buckets in horror. A wall had collapsed on my parents before they could get out.

Blinking away the vision and a few tears, I heard a whimper and look down to see Megs, my German Shepherd. My mood changed from sad to happy and a bit of pride as I knelt down and scratched behind her ears. Looking into her big brown eyes, I remembered being a sixteen-year-old girl finding the little pup in a box hiding from the rain. She was in the same state I used to be: cold, hungry and wet. I kept her and raised her, she proving to be a worthy companion and one of the best trained dogs in the King's pack.

Thinking of my family brought back the memory of my precious little sister, Hanna. She was the only one I could save from the burning house. I had to give her to my mother's friend who could give her a regular life without the burden of knowing our parents were dead. I made the woman promise not to tell Hanna the truth until she was old enough to handle it, that she would raise Hanna as her own. When she swore to do so, I handed Hanna to her, kissed her on the forehead, and ran off, not looking back because if I did, I would've regretted it forever. Though, I didn't leave without giving Hanna something of our mother's.

A knock on the door and Megs' bark jerked me back to the present. Hiding my ring under my shirt, I opened the door and standing there was my best friend, Melissa, but I called her Millie. Queen Veronica introduced us not long after I arrived at the castle. She thought that Millie would help influence me to be more like the proper princess I *ought to have been*. Those plans didn't work out the way she expected either, for I influenced Millie just as much as she influenced me. We were best friends ever since, both having accepted each other fairly quickly.

"Hey, Millie," I greeted.

"Hello, Sam!" Millie stated excitedly, her eyes practically bulging out of her head.

"What's got you all piped up?" I couldn't help but smile. Millie had a way of making people do that. She was such a smiley person with a bright personality; a very likable girl.

"The King is holding a joust and wants you to participate in the competition," she said in her usual perky voice. She knew me well.

"Millie," I stated as I grabbed my sword, "let's go show those knights what Sam the Lion Heart can do!"

"Yay!" Millie exclaimed as she jumped up and down whilst clapping her hands. This made me throw my head back and laugh so hard that Millie couldn't help but blush.

"Ouch!" I shouted, "Not so tight. I'm not a girl!"

"Sorry, Will," John muttered.

John tried to put my armor on me with great care. He wasn't doing as good as usual. Typically very good at knowing just how tight to fasten the breastplate and which piece of armor goes on when, today he seemed anxious. Something must have bothered him.

17

"What is it, John? Are you nervous?" I asked.

"No," John said. "It's just…"

"Oh, so you *are* nervous!" I pestered him.

"I am not! It's just…"

"It's just what?"

"Well," he stammered, "you are going to battle someone you're not familiar with."

"Why would you be nervous about that?" I asked, "Who is it?"

"You will be jousting Sam the Lion Heart… and I am *not* nervous!"

"Alright, alright, whatever you say," I laughed. "And what makes you think this *Sam the Lion Heart* is any different from any other knight?"

"Well, Sam the Lion Heart hasn't lost a single joust."

My laughing suddenly turned to coughing then silence. How could someone not lose a single joust? I mean, I'd won a lot of jousts, but I'd lost some too. Not losing a single joust was impossible. I couldn't let John see that now I was a tad bit nervous. That would only make it worse.

"Well, John," I assured, forcing a smile, "looks like this will be Sam's first loss."

Most other knights had squires to put armor on their masters for them, but since I was the only female knight around and no other girl wanted to be a knight, I didn't have a squire, and I had to dress myself. The knight who trained me, Sir Hugh, made that very clear when I was still learning.

I supposed Millie could've helped me, but she wasn't very interested in such things. Besides, I learned how to put on my own armor before I fully knew her.

As if right on cue, the door swung open and in leapt Millie, bouncing up and down as she screamed, "Sam! Sam! Guess what, guess what, *guess what*?"

"Hmm, let me think. The world is round?" I teased her.

She stopped jumping and grew serious, which looked awfully funny since she was usually smiling. "*No*, you know that's impossible," she stated mater of factly.

"Alright, a square then?" I smiled.

Millie only sighed in annoyance.

"Oh come on, Millie. Can't you take a joke?" I laughed, "Alright, what is it?"

Millie rolled her eyes and said as I pulled my boots on, "Ha ha, very funny. Anyway, you'll be competing against someone new at the joust."

"Looks like I'll be showing another knight what this girl can do," I replied with a tinge of sarcasm as I tied off my leather bracers and pulled on my gauntlets, grabbing my helmet and sword before I turned to look back at my friend. "Who is this knight?"

"He's called William of the Silver Blade."

I recognized the name. As I recalled, he was one of the knights entrusted to look after a portion of Etheland. I had not met him before since he hadn't been Master of his territory for too long. But being in charge of such land, he must've been one of the top knights in the King's army, a Great Knight. Of course, I had beaten the best before, so this shouldn't be any different. Besides, jousting was an easy sport, not too much combat involved, only the ability to hold

19

a lance and dodge any blows. And as far as I knew, the King only organized a simple joust, not a full-fledged entertaining spectacle.

"Sounds like a worthy opponent. Good luck to him." I threw my sword in the air with a grin. "He's going to need it." As we walked out the door, I caught my sword in midair and slid it in its sheath. "Come, Megs. This is going to be quite a game."

Chapter Two

"That's him," John said, pointing. "That's Sam the Lion Heart."

I turned my head to see a young man in full armor. I couldn't see what he looked like for he had his helmet on, but I heard his name so much that I had the strangest feeling that I heard it sometime before the tournament. It could just be my head playing tricks on me, but it still itched at the back of my mind like there was some piece of information trying to make itself known.

"It's almost time for you to begin," John's words brought me from my own thoughts. I nodded as I got up on my horse. "Your lance," John said as he humbly presented the giant colored stick to me. I grabbed it, raised it and waited for the signal.

Glancing over to the other side of the arena, I saw my opponent, William of the Silver Blade. He was tall with brown locks of hair. He appeared handsome, but one should never judge a book by its cover. Looking through the slits of my helm, I noticed that he was looking at me. Of course he couldn't recognize me as my better known title, could he? No, he couldn't. At that moment, he only knew me as Sam the Lion Heart. Most never made the connection between my titles; not realizing until much later that all my identities were but one person.

Almost time for my turn, I climbed onto my horse, Autumn, and lifted my lance. I watched as William pulled his helm down over his head, covering his face, making him hardly recognizable.

The flag dropped. I pressed my heels into Autumn's sides and she broke into a run. I loved the feeling of the wind in my face—well, the parts of my face it could get to—the pounding of my heart and the tight grip on my lance. As William came close, I grit my teeth, narrowed my eyes, and gave a sharp yell as my lance pounded against my opponent's chest, exploding in a shower of splinters, causing him to topple off of his horse and land on the ground hard. The round was up; William had fallen quickly and I won.

"Oh," I groaned as I grasped my chest with one arm and blocked my fall with the other. My shoulder rang as the impact jarred my arm, the rest of my body crashing to the ground in suit.

What happened? It was all so fast. One minute I was excited and full of energy, the next I was falling off my horse! Allowing my helm to slip off my head, I opened my eyes as the knight jumped off his mare. The pain in my chest started to gradually weaken. My opponent reached for his helm and lifted it off his head.

I gasped. John gasped. I heard everyone who had traveled with me gasp. I expected to see a big, tough *Sam the Lion Heart*, but no, I stared at not a man, but a woman. *Samantha.* I could tell why she was called Sam the Lion Heart. She was obviously brave and fearless, but most of all, I expected she got such a title from her hair. Wavy and fiery red, it seemed to glow like flames in the sunlight. Her pale blue eyes cast down on me gave a shocking contrast to the red of her hair. I could hardly speak from the surprise.

The announcer shouted loudly for all to hear, "And the winner is Princess Samantha!" Sam gave a sharp look at the announcer and his expression looked suddenly scared as he corrected himself, "Pardon, Highness, I meant, Sam the Lion Heart!"

Wait a moment. *Princess* Samantha? I lost not only to a girl, but to the Princess? The thought in the back of my head finally made a clear appearance in my mind's eye. I remembered the hushed buzz in my household a few years ago of a woman being knighted by the King, the first woman to be so. I never thought much of it, for most things like that were but rumors. Clearly they were true. Not only was it a woman who was knighted, but the Princess herself!

As I tried to take it all in, Sam came over to where I still lay from my fall. She rested her elbow on her knee as she knelt down, saying loud enough for only me to hear, "Well, to be honest, I was expecting more from you. Now, listen to me very closely, William…."

"Will," I corrected her.

"Will." She didn't seem to care. "Now that you know who I really am, I must tell you something: if you ever, *ever*, call me Samantha or even *think* to call me Samantha," she paused as if to see if I was paying attention, "you'll regret it."

Sam took my hand, yanked me up and walked away so fast that I hardly believed it all actually happened. If it weren't for the sudden pain in my shoulder from the force in which she pulled me up, I wouldn't have believed it at all.

John ran up to me. "Will! Are you all right?"

"Yeah." I stared after Sam, rubbing my sore shoulder. I certainly didn't expect a woman to have such strength. Now my shoulder hurt as much as my chest, maybe even worse.

Chapter Three

Brushing the twigs and grime off of Autumn, I couldn't help but notice how every time I brushed one section, it came out a silky, shiny chestnut color. She looked exceptionally bright today—probably due to the victory at the tournament yesterday. Touching the white star on her forehead, my hand traveled down to finger the white spot on her heal, a sign of good fortune. Autumn whinnied and pushed her head against mine. Giggling softly, I stroked her long neck, soft and smooth. As the sound of the stable door opened behind me, Autumn jerked back slightly and I turned my head around to see who entered. It was my mother, Queen Veronica.

The way she held herself was regal even in the stables. Her dark eyes ventured around until they fixed on me. She didn't seem to pay much heed to the earthy smell of the horses, nor did she bother to lift her long skirts over the straw that littered the floor. It wouldn't have mattered anyway. Even if she pinched her nose and lifted her skirts above her ankles, the aroma would still fill her nostrils and pieces of straw would still cling to the rich fabric. At least the Queen's light, gray streaked hair was pinned up and out of the way.

"Hello, Samantha," Queen Veronica greeted me with a fair smile.

"Hello, Mother," I said softly as I turned to calm my horse though she hardly needed it.

"Oh," the Queen sighed as she stroked Autumn's neck, "I have always admired your horse."

I suppressed a smile. The Queen usually only used such a tone when she wanted something. "What is it?" I questioned.

"Must you always think I want something when I am simply admiring your horse?"

I turned back and continued to brush my horse, smiling to myself. Queen Veronica didn't say anything, so I didn't either. After a while, I suspected she couldn't handle the silence.

"Samantha, honey?"

Pet names assured the fact that she wanted something from me. Compliments were normal, but such names like *honey* and *sweetheart* not so much. It betrayed how she thought strategically before she spoke. She wasn't one to use such names in every day speech, but the Queen thought it was something a mother would say to her daughter, so when she thought about it, she used the names. Of course, who was I to oppose her using them when she was deprived of a child until I came along? I almost thought that the Queen believed that using the names helped me as if reminding me that I had a mother still. I didn't need such things to remind me that I had a mother. Still, even after all these years, it felt good to know that she still tried.

"Yes?" I responded.

"There is a ball this evening and I would like you to attend. Will you come?" Queen Veronica questioned. I knew this was meant as more of a request than a choice, the question spoken out of mere politeness.

I sighed, smiling teasingly at her. "Do I have a choice?"

She quickly lit up. "Fantastic! Oh, and you *are* going to wear an actual gown."

This was a regular demand at such events. Queen Veronica was afraid that I'd show up at a royal ball in men's clothes. I stifled a giggle at the thought of the Queen's face if that happened, but I always wore an appropriate gown for such occasions, though I typically stayed well out of sight. Balls had never been my favorite. They were overcrowded and I felt out of place at such formal events. Millie tried to get me into the festivity of parties, but it never worked. I usually just watched and laughed as my best friend was swept away by suitors.

Queen Veronica said a few more lines on how spectacular the ball would be, insisting that this time I'd have a grand time. I only nodded and smiled as I continued to groom my mare, knowing that the social life of royalty was not a place I fit in well. The Queen soon took leave after requesting that I did the same soon so I had plenty of time to get ready.

Polishing my sword, my mind wandered to the events of yesterday. I still couldn't believe that I lost to the Princess. It would be embarrassing if I'd lost to just a regular girl, but the *Princess*? Well, I supposed God never said that men were better than women or women were better than men. Perhaps I shouldn't be embarrassed about being beaten by her. Besides, a lot of other knights had been as well, or so I was told. She'd never lost, so I couldn't be the first.

The door creaked open behind me and a young man stood in the doorway with a scroll in his hands. By his attire, I could tell he was a scribe; the King's scribe by way of the fineness of the fabric.

"Sir William," pronounced the scribe, "the King and Queen would like to invite you and your company to a royal ball this evening. What shall I inform His Majesty?"

I thought but a moment before I responded, "My company and I would be honored to attend the royal ball."

The scribe bowed before hurriedly exiting the room without a word. After a while I left as well. I had to go get John. There was a ball to get ready for after all.

Opening the door, I found none other than Millie, a sly smile spread over her flushed face. Clearly she'd been running for she was panting heavily, still trying to catch her breath.

"Won't you come in?" I joked.

Millie didn't seem to catch my comment. "So," she went on to say, "I hear there's a ball tonight."

"Oh, please don't tell me you're excited about this ball, too," I interrupted.

"Fine, I won't say it, but since there *is* a ball and you're going to it, I came up to help you get ready." She grinned widely, visibly excited.

"Hmm, let me think." I put on my best thoughtful face, trying to hide how much I wanted to smile at my friend's enthusiasm.

"Oh, come on, Sam! Please, please, please, please, *please*!" Millie nearly screamed. She stuck out her lip, batted her long eye lashes, and softly said, "Please, for me?"

"Awe, you know I can't say no to your puppy face," I giggled. "But I get a say on the outfit."

Millie immediately brightened up. "Yay!" she squealed as she ran up and gave me a tight hug.

"Millie! I can't breathe!" I gasped. I knew I could easily pry out of her arms, but Millie needed to keep some of her pride.

"Oops, sorry," Millie apologized as she let go. "Alright, time to choose our dresses!" I groaned as she pulled me out the door.

Walking down the hall with John, we just came back from asking my company if they would like to attend the King's ball. Practically everyone accepted. Of course, John said yes, too. He loved this kind of thing. Always the liveliest at the parties back home; this would be his first royal ball, so he was doubly excited.

I remembered my first ball. I was very young, almost too young to attend such an event. My parents were Masters of

29

our home at the time and only just under the royal family in authority, so I was permitted to attend. My mother taught me how to dance beforehand. The other women I danced with seemed amused by me being such a young partner and most even helped me learn different steps. I expected it was quite a spectacle, for I wasn't always the best at the moves. At least I hoped I improved since then. Mother seemed to think so, anyway, before... I couldn't allow my mind to travel down that road. I focused on the now as John and I were off to get ready.

I couldn't seem to get Sam out of my head! The one thing that particularly haunted me were those eyes, eyes that burned with fearlessness, passion and so much more behind them that didn't make sense. I recognized it even in my brief time with her: pain and heartbreak. How could a princess, who could have anything she wanted without even raising a finger, have such hurt in her eyes? Shrugging it off, I decided that I needed to focus on one thing at a time. At that moment, it was the King's ball.

John and I walked swiftly, and as we turned the corner we found a huge and very painful surprise.

A sudden collision made my head ring and I found myself sprawled out on the floor, my hair in my face and someone atop me! Millie gasped in surprise and another more masculine voice gasped as well. I blew the hair out of my face and ended up staring right into a pair of green eyes. Recognition dawned on me. William?

He stared at me in shock. Well, I guess I was staring at him too, but I had no choice; he wouldn't get off me! What was his excuse for staring? Heat rose to my face. There wasn't that much to stare at. There were, after all, a whole lot of better things to stare at—like Millie. At least, from what I observed, most guys tended to stare at her much more than me.

Will, unlike me, was worth staring at. Wavy brown hair, shining green eyes—not light green, not dark green, just green— he was tall and muscular. I mean, not the extreme muscular, but the normal and fit muscular. I supposed he was pretty handsome.

Wait a minute! What was I thinking? Besides, Will still wouldn't stop gawking and hadn't gotten off of me. I tried to resist the urge to shove him off, so instead I said, "Would you mind?" which came out a little harsher than I intended.

Will blinked as if waking from shock. "Oh, right. Sorry."

Holding out his hand as he stood, I ignored the gesture and got up by myself, quickly slipping my ring under my shirt so it didn't peek out anymore.

"Sorry," he apologized again.

"It's fine." I shrugged. "Everyone crashes into each other at this corner. That's why it's called Crash Corner."

"Really?" Will looked surprised.

"No," I said flatly. Millie stifled back a laugh.

Obviously embarrassed, he said, "I guess I'll see you tonight."

"Fine," I said, suddenly spiteful.

I walked around him, my belly tightening and my back stiff. I wasn't sure if I liked this William of the Silver Blade or not. He seemed like any other man the Queen had introduced me to before, though toned down much more than those other knights.

Queen Veronica used to look for suitable nobles as suitors for me, but gave up long ago after a particularly frustrating engagement with the son of a neighboring Duke of Lynnia. She exclaimed that if I wished to die alone then so be it! Since then, she stopped inviting flirtatious suitors who were only interested because I was a princess.

I didn't always rebel against Queen Veronica, but I was very firm on the belief that if I was to marry, it would be to the man who I chose and who chose me for who I was, not what I was. Thankfully, the Queen seemed to have accepted that. She just prayed that such a man would soon meet my acquaintance. Frankly, I was afraid that day wouldn't come for quite some time, if at all. William would just end up like the rest of them.

Once Will and his friend were out of sight, my knees felt weak and I leaned on Millie to regain my balance.

Chapter Four

As John and I strode down one of the many halls within the castle, the back of my neck prickled with the vague sense of someone watching me. I fought the urge to turn around and give away my suspicions. Thus, I decided to make use of having John beside me, hoping I did not act too out of character.

"Tell me something, John," I started, glancing down at him since he was a head shorter than me.

"What?" he inquired.

"Anything really," I replied, lowering my voice. "Just so long as it looks like we are having a conversation."

"We are having a conversation."

"I mean, something lighthearted," I suggested, "something humorous."

John pondered a moment, before muttering, "If I do, will you explain what's going on?"

"Of course, but be quick," I urged, my suspicions rising by the second.

"How could you even think such a thing would work?" John questioned suddenly, raising his voice instantly.

His quickness set me back, and I had to force my expression not to look too startled at his shadowed accusation. Unsure how exactly to respond, I guffawed, "From my standpoint, I believe it could've worked!"

"You're not all that great of a jumper, no matter how long your legs are." John shook his head with a believable exasperated laugh.

"I'd like to see you do better!" I found myself proclaiming, opening my arms as if welcoming him to whatever challenge he was initiating.

"All I'm saying is that next time you want to leap over a river, don't call for me to fetch you out." He smirked mischievously.

As the conversation became clearer in my mind, I gave a loud laugh and turned around to walk backwards before John. "What real harm can come of a bit of water in your socks?" I questioned playfully.

"You never know what real trouble you're in until the water's above your head and find the current's too strong," John insisted.

I didn't hear what else he went on to say, my attentions turned elsewhere. Sneaking my gaze beyond my friend, only a blur of brown fabric caught my eye and a white kerchief lay on the ground in the middle of the hall. My brow furrowed in confusion, but there was nothing else to see. The follower was gone.

"Will," John hissed.

With a start, I turned back to my friend, but he was not looking at me. His gaze was fixed on something just behind me.

"Sir William, is it?" a stately voice questioned.

Turning, I found myself in the presence of Queen Veronica herself, two attendants trailing behind her. With a tinge of clumsiness, I hastened to stoop in a short bow. "You are most accurate, Your Highness."

John bowed in a similar fashion, though his was far more graceful. The Queen's dark eyes regarded us in an almost amused manner.

"I do hope I have not interrupted anything of importance," she stated. "I know how difficult it must be when you are away from the affairs of your own estate."

"No, nothing of importance to interrupt, Your Majesty," I assured. "And it is true of the concerns of being away, but I have my full confidence in Sir Levi that he will run everything without much difficulty until I return."

"Well spoken," the Queen complimented. "I am most certain of your good judgment. Sir Levi is as fine a man as any who once fought alongside my husband. And I trust that your own reign as Master over those lands has proved well entrusted?"

"I believe it has, Highness," I assured. "I can only strive to live up to my father's wisdom."

"Yes, your father was a good man and just ruler," she agreed. "I was much saddened upon hearing of his passing, as well as that of your mother's. Though I am many years late in saying such, my condolences go to you, Sir William."

"Thank you, Your Highness." I stooped my head in a grateful gesture.

"Yes, well I do hope that you gentlemen enjoy yourselves this evening," Queen Veronica continued. "A ball is an excellent way to take one's mind off solemn matters."

"I couldn't agree more." I smiled politely.

With a nod of farewell, the Queen continued on down the hall, leaving John and me alone. His face instantly fell into one of confused concern.

"Care to explain what that was about?" he questioned, indicating the event before the Queen showed up.

"Well, it's like you said, John," I stated, retrieving the fallen kerchief that caused my suspicions to peak. "You never know what real trouble you're in until the water's above your head and find the current's too strong."

"I don't like this one," I exclaimed to Millie. "It's so tight, yet puffy and plump! How is that even possible?"

Millie's eyes wandered over the dress I tried on, her face scrunched up in thought. She motioned for me to turn around. Wobbling about, I found great difficulty in making a circle. The dress was bright and yellow with emeralds sewn into the trim, making it heavier. It had bulging sleeves and a skirt with about fifty petticoats that made my hips seem much wider than they actually were. The corset caused me to fight for breath.

"Yeah, I think this one looks… what's the word?" Millie thought out loud.

"Hideous!" I suggested with a huff.

"Yes, that's it!"

"Does that mean I can take this beast of a dress off now?"

"Please," she laughed.

I ripped off the corset and gasped for breath. Oh, air, precious air!

Millie looked at me curiously, moving closer. "What's this?" she asked, taking the ring around my neck to examine it closer. The chain tightening, I bent over so as not to strangle myself. "You still wear it?" Millie questioned incredulously, "Close to your heart, just like you used to?"

"Of course I do," I responded, gingerly retrieving the ring from Millie's grasp. "It was my mother's."

"Oh, Sam," she sighed dreamily. "You have no idea how sentimentally, beautifully tragic you are."

"Uh, thanks?"

"It's a good thing. Most people don't have stories worth being told such as yours, even if it is a tragic one." Millie examined me. "Unfortunately, you can't wear that around your neck this evening."

"Why?" I questioned.

"Jewels, Sam. Jewels," she stated matter-of-factly. "You're going to have to wear it on your finger, like a normal ring."

I sighed, pulling the chain over my head and sliding the ring off. Almost hesitantly, I slipped the ring on my right ring finger. It fit. At least it would stay there for the ball, though it was strange not having it close to my heart.

"Excellent!" my friend cried. "Now, about the dress…"

Placing the chain in Millie's outstretched hand, I asked the seamstress, "Do you have anything that's fitting and loose in the skirts, with three petticoats maximum?"

"I believe I have just the thing," the seamstress answered. She rummaged through the closet and pulled out a dress.

My eyes imminently lit up. "Perfect."

Standing in the middle of the ball room, watching, John already found a partner to dance with which didn't surprise me. There were so many different people. The oddest outfit I'd seen so far was a bright yellow puffy dress with emeralds sewn into the trim worn by a large woman. Her partner matched.

I didn't know where Sam was, nor why I found myself so anxious to see her. Perhaps I just wanted to see the way she looked in the form of a princess instead of a knight. I didn't know. My gut felt peculiar at the thought of her. I wasn't sure if I liked it. *She should be here*, my mind nagged. The wonder of where she could be wouldn't leave me alone.

Whispers rippled through the crowd and the violins screeched, hastily trying to pick up the melody again. I turned around sharply to see Sam at the top of the staircase. She hardly looked at all the way I saw her last. She appeared just as stunning as before, even if it was in a different and new way. Her elegant pale blue gown—a similar color to that of her eyes—was trimmed with a hint of silver thread. A silver sash wrapped round her waist, draping in the front. Simple jewelry adorned her neck and a little gold ring with an emerald embedded in the fine metal was the only thing decorating her hands. Some of Sam's hair was braided up while the rest of it fell down her back like waves, ending at her waist.

John walked up behind me and asked, "Is that Sam?"

"Yes," I responded, reluctantly taking my eyes off her as she descended the staircase. The music back up again at its normal pace, everyone acted as their normal state of enjoyment.

"Why don't you ask her to dance? I can tell you want to," John persisted.

"I don't know, John. I mean, just yesterday we were jousting."

"Well, you know what they say: joust one day and dance the next."

"Who says that?" I questioned.

"Me, just now," he replied with a big grin.

"Alright, you got me." I choked back laughter. Making my way to the Princess, I almost lost heart when she stood next to Queen Veronica and King Richard. I continued on anyway, though. John would never let me forget it if I backed out now.

This was a mistake. I shouldn't have come. I twisted my ring now on my finger around and around nervously. I hated being the center of attention like this. I would, if permitted, disappear into the crowd and become invisible for the rest of the day. Or I'd find Millie and spend time with her. I could sometimes find enjoyment in these balls with my best friend, but I had to stay with the King and Queen for a while as a sign of respect before I could vanish.

"You look lovely, dear," Queen Veronica whispered, moving closer to my side so as we could communicate without drawing attention.

I sighed softly, my nose and cheeks heating. I never felt comfortable when told such compliments on my appearance. I whispered back my usual response, "Beauty should not be determined by the outward appearance."

She smiled softly, dark eyes shining. "Of course not, but sometimes beauty can shine from the inside out."

My face grew even warmer. I sensed someone approaching; a prickle ran up my spine. Turning around, I spied Will moving my way. I wondered if it was merely coincidence, but soon discarded the thought as he stopped right in front of the royal couple and me. He bowed deeply before the King and then to the Queen. My chest pressurized when he bowed to me. I hated such formalities made to me. It felt wrong.

A slight blush rose in his cheeks. "May I have the honor of having this dance, Your Highness?"

Stunned, I wondered if I heard him correctly. This man must have been either brave or just plain stupid. No, I wasn't over exaggerating. My eyes drifted to the Queen. She gave a slight nod. I slightly shook my head, my eyes widening.

She only smiled wider and, turning to Will, said, "My daughter would love to dance."

When he looked to me, I forced my face to seem relaxed. I even managed a slight smile, though my stomach was in sudden knots. He extended his hand and I reluctantly accepted.

Will, still holding my hand, led me to the middle of the dance floor. Neither of us said anything; neither of us really wished to. When at last he turned to me, he was almost tentative about placing his hand around my waist, but he did so anyway. I was sure that from the outside, the two of us seemed like any other couple waiting for the upcoming dance. Inside, however, I felt as if a confusion of heat and knots befuddled my brain and gut. The music started a slow song and Will and I glided across the dance floor.

She was so uneasy, tense. Then again, so was I. Thankfully, I could dance automatically as my mind drew a blank. As we moved across the floor towards the fireplace, I noticed her eyes flick to the fire. She froze. Her breath came short as if in a panic. I quickly guided her away from the fireplace and she started to relax.

"Are you all right?" I asked.

"Yes, I'm fine." Sam nodded, smiling softly as if to forget the matter.

My mind wandered. Why didn't Sam want to be near the fire? Was she afraid? I tossed that thought aside. No, she couldn't be. But still...

Sam twirled and her skirt flowed around her in glassy blue waves. We came back together and I dipped her. As I brought her back up, our eyes locked. My mind went empty again and I felt almost frozen in that pale blue gaze. Neither of us moved. It was as if time itself stopped for that one brief second. She seemed so calm, vulnerable, her eyes revealing the discomfort and nervousness that had been concealed just moments before. The tightness in my gut seemed to unknot and relax itself, the blank state of my mind clearing. In an instant, a curtain fell over her eyes once more and the same intense blaze filled them again. The song ended and she pulled away, giving a quick curtsy before she walked off, disappearing into the crowd.

Chapter Five

I fingered my ring, now in its proper place on the chain around my neck. Sleep didn't come, my mind much too active for rest. Too many confusing thoughts, too many strange emotions. I didn't know what had gotten into me tonight. My legs felt jittery; my hands wished to be busy. Antsy, I just felt so antsy.

Kicking off the blankets, my feet dropped to the cold floor. Quickly, I found my shoes so I didn't freeze my toes and pulled on my clothes. I put pillows on my bed so that it looked as if I was still there, just in case someone came in to check on me. No one ever had before, but I could never be too sure. Grabbing my knife, I stuck it in its sheath and put it in my climbing boots. Making sure not to wake anyone, I opened the door, stepped into the hall, and softly closed it behind me.

My feet, being used to sneaking around without making a sound, easily glided through the hall without so much as a peep. As I walked by the King and Queen's bed chamber, I choked back a laugh. King Richard snored so loudly from inside, the noise vibrated in the silence. It was amazing that Queen Veronica could sleep a wink! Going slowly down the hall at first, I gradually went faster and faster. I made my way down the staircase leading to the guest rooms' floor.

Quietly and quickly I traveled, for I didn't know if the guests were heavy sleepers that slumbered on through a raging storm or light sleepers that woke at the slightest noise. My pace quickened to a near run, growing steadily faster. My foot slipped straight behind me and I fell, landing sprawled on the floor with a heavy thud. Looking back, I took note that I tripped over something hairy and white: a wig.

It must have been midnight by now. I still couldn't sleep! Everyone else was, or at least the men who'd come with me were. I could hear their soft breathing and occasional snore of their dreaming... whatever kinds of dreams they were having. But my mind wouldn't quit racing after the events that transpired today, what with the ball and the strange encounters with Sam and the Queen, as well as the person who had followed me that afternoon. The kerchief was on the table by my bed, sitting like a ghost in the night.

John suddenly jolted up in his bed. "No! Don't leave! Don't leave me all alone!"

I reached out to comfort him. "Don't worry, John. It was only a dream."

He nodded his head slowly in fatigue and mumbled, "Right, right. It was only a... a dream." He then collapsed onto his pillow and immediately fell into the rhythmic breathing one does when asleep.

An out of place thud sounded in the silence, causing me to nearly jump out of my skin! What was that? An image of the blurred pursuer crossed my mind and a sinking feeling filled my stomach. Getting out of bed, I quickly yanked on some clothes and made my way gingerly past the sleeping men to the door. Opening it a crack, I peeped out.

Once my eyes adjusted to the dark, I realized in surprise that it was Sam! What was she doing out and about so late? Well, I supposed I should probably ask myself the same question. She got up from the floor carefully and walked down the hall as quietly and delicately as a cat. I opened the door, stepped out and shut it quietly behind me. Not knowing why I did it, I followed after Sam, the sudden urge to know where she's going and what she's up to tickled my brain.

The Princess and I whipped around corners and traveled down numerous stairs until I found myself in a garden walled off by the castle barriers. Sam went up to the wall and easily climbed up and over it. I followed, though with much more difficulty. Finally, after I was over the wall, I had the split and sudden panic that I lost Sam. My gaze scoured over the outskirts of the village before me. Finally, I spotted a figure with red hair jump up onto a building not far from here. Again with less agility as she, I made my way after her.

Following her over various buildings and roof tops, I looked down and noticed how we seemed to be getting farther out of the wealthier part of town. Slate roofing turned to wood and straw. It was getting poorer and messier down on the ground. We finally made it so we were both on the street, though I didn't know how. My eyes stayed fixed on Sam so I wouldn't get lost. Without warning, she whipped around a corner, and, of course, I pursued.

Something rammed into my stomach, showering my vision with spots. Starting to double over in pain at the sudden blow, I was thrust against the wall and an arm held me in place. Next thing I knew, the cold edge of a knife touched my throat and a silky voice said between clenched teeth, "Why are you following me?"

What did he think he was doing, trailing after me like that? A furious annoyance with him tightened in my throat. Though, it was a little satisfying to see Will's fear stricken face with a tinge of shock.

I formed my voice in the same tone as before, "What are you doing here?"

"I guess I should ask the same to you, Princess," he said with surprising courage. "What are *you* doing here?"

"I asked you first," I retorted, my voice as thick as honey.

"I wanted to see what you were up to." Will cocked his head slightly away from the knife blade. "Your turn, Princess."

I glared at him. "Don't call me *princess*."

"But you are one, aren't you, Princess?"

Feeling as if about to burst, I shouted, "Do *not* call me a princess!"

His face fell, obviously taken back by my outburst. I scowled at him. "You want to know what I'm doing here? Fine! I'll show you."

With that, I reluctantly slid my knife back in its sheath, turned around and stomped off. I didn't even check to see if he followed. I could hear his unaccustomed feet stumbling and slipping on the uneven ground, trying to keep up with my fast pace.

Chapter Six

What Sam had said made no sense to me. Why did she despise being called princess so much? She was one, after all. She should have been used to the title; she was the King and Queen's daughter. Maybe I shouldn't have spoken that way. I didn't know why I did it. She could have slit my throat at any given moment, after all.

I slipped again for the umpteenth time. This time, I didn't fall completely on the floor. My neck heats anyway, embarrassed at how spoiled I'd become with my estate's even floors. Sam continued to lead me through dark allies and around houses, or at least what could be called houses.

My mind flitted to a long ago memory, one I often shoved away. It was of two young men, one of whom was me, venturing in a place very similar to this. Except, the paths had been of dirt and grass, the houses made of wood and branches. The buildings here could be replaced by trees there, many trees, and instead of a town, it had been more of a sanctuary. I pushed aside the vision from before as I always did.

Focusing on the present, my feet became more accustomed to the strange style of pavement. Sam soon stopped in front of an old, shabby hut, though flowers grew about its base as if to make up for the poverty of the building. What was a princess doing in a place like this?

"Wait here." I held Will back before I knocked on the door and waited.

The door opened a crack, and a woman peeped out. "Who is it?" she asked.

"Sam," I responded.

The woman widened her eyes in recognition and opened the door wider, her vision apparently having accustomed to the dark. Now visible, her fair hair gleamed in the light from the inside.

I greeted the woman, "Hello, Elizabeth." Noticing a bundle in Elizabeth's arms, my eyes widened. "Did you have your baby?"

She nodded with a smile on her face. "It's a girl: Samantha." Elizabeth looked down on her daughter with affection. She named her baby after me! My face burned with pride.

A blond boy of nine years peeped from behind her skirt, his blue eyes shining.

I smiled. "Hello, Owen. Missed me?"

A grin crept up on his rosy face. Owen ran up and gave me a tackle of a hug. I ruffled my hand through his blond locks teasingly.

As I was squeezed by Owen, Elizabeth shook her head. "They hear your name and they come running, even after bed."

"Can we stay up, *please*?" Owen begged, smiling wide as he hung his head upside down while tugging on my arm.

She sighed, amused, "Only for a little while."

Owen laughed joyfully. Just now, another little rosy faced figure peeked out from behind Elizabeth's skirt.

I smiled warmly. "Hello, Isabel."

As she came out from the other side of her mother, she smiled shyly and gave a little curtsy before she too ran up and gave me a hug. Her hair was fair like her mother's, lighter than Owen's, but her eyes were almond colored like her father's.

Elizabeth glanced over my shoulder. "Who is this?"

I acknowledged Will standing behind me, "Oh, this is Will."

Elizabeth looked him up and down, her gaze soon flicking between the two of us. "And are you two…"

I instantly shook my head in surprise. "What? No, we're just…"

"Friends," Will butt in.

I glared back at him and said between clenched teeth, "Actually, I was going to say *acquaintances*, but I guess *friends* will do."

Elizabeth gave a nod of understanding. "Well, do come in. It's cold outside."

Owen and Isabel ran into the hut, dragging me in with them.

As the woman called Elizabeth closed the door softly behind me, I took a look around the room. The house was small with not a lot of unnecessary furnishings. Two doors led off to different rooms, one I assumed to be the main bedroom whilst the other was most likely the pantry or privy. This room appeared to be the main living space, acting as the kitchen, washing room, dining space, and bedroom for the children. There was only one window as far as I could see. All in all, it was a pretty cozy hut. Well, as cozy as huts went.

"Sam," the young girl pleaded as she tugged on the Princess' shirt hem, "may I play with your hair, please?"

Sam smiled warmly down at her. "Sure, if you'd like."

Isabel jumped up with a little squeal of joy. She ran over to a trunk beside the bunk bed and brought back a brush. Pulling a chair up, she beckoned Sam to sit. Once seated, Isabel started to gently brush through the silky red flames of Sam's hair.

Elizabeth brought up two more chairs in front of Sam and gestured for me to sit. Obliging, I nodded towards Isabel. "How old is she?"

"Six years," Elizabeth replied as she sat in the other chair, still clutching her baby.

Owen came up and sat on the floor in the center of the triangle of chairs, his big blue eyes staring intently at me. It seemed as if he was studying me, trying to decide what to think.

Sam then asked, "Where's Ulric?"

Elizabeth looked up. "He is at the Brown's helping with the milking while Mister Brown is out of town for work. With Mrs. Brown ill, the poor thing, it was the least Ulric could do to help. I would've gone, too, but I have to stay here and take care of this lot."

"Mrs. Brown is ill?" Sam's tone revealed her concern.

"With a head cold, but she's recovering." Elizabeth turned to me. "Ulric is my husband, just so you know."

I nodded in understanding.

Isabel threw up her hands and exclaimed, "Done!"

"Thank you, Isabel. I'm sure it looks lovely." Sam smiled.

The child's face glowed with pride. I noticed Sam fingering something around her neck, but when I took a closer look, she eyed me and tucked it under her shirt.

"And how is Cousin Nancy?" Elizabeth asked.

"Oh, she is as happy as ever, being engaged and all. She's extremely excited for the wedding," Sam said.

"Oh, that's good. How is the cottage coming along?"

"It's coming. Garrick has been working mighty hard on it so that it will be ready once they're married."

Having no idea who the two women are talking about, I could only listen and nod. Being sure to hang onto every word, I hoped their conversation would reveal some interesting factors about Sam, perhaps even answer some of my questions and wonderings without meaning to do such.

Owen jumped up quickly, asking Sam, "Can you show me how to use my bow and arrow?"

"Dear me, no!" Elizabeth exclaimed, "It is far past your bed times! Off to bed, now."

Owen and Isabel both gave a pouty face.

"Maybe next time, alright Owen?" Sam suggested. "Besides, we should probably get going. I just wanted to check in on you."

"Oh, you do so much already," Elizabeth proclaimed.

Owen, after having stared at me for quite some time, came up and whispered, "I think I like you."

I whispered back, "I think I like you, too."

He grinned before running off to his bed. Isabel shyly smiled at me before going off as well. Elizabeth and Sam embraced each other and exchanged their good-byes. I stood up also, not expecting the hug I got from Elizabeth.

"Good-bye. It was nice meeting you," Elizabeth said as she pulled away.

"And you as well," I responded. I glanced down at the baby Samantha in her arms. I saw why they named her that: fiery red hair.

Leading the way, I heard Will tripping and slipping behind, his feet not used to the terribly laid pavement yet. A silence lay between us as if neither wishes to utter a word to disturb it. I didn't care. I wasn't sure I wanted to hear his voice just yet anyway.

Never the less, he spoke, "How do you know them?"

I stopped dead in my tracks, causing him to almost bump into me. My mind automatically veered back to the time I rescued Elizabeth and Owen. My own screams rang in my head. The shadow of pain licked at my back. I didn't enjoy remembering this part, though typically I found consolation in what happened after. Strangely, I couldn't now, as if my mind wouldn't allow access to the rest of my memory.

Once Will recovered his balance, he asked again, "How do you know them? Why does it offend you to be called a princess? Why do you come out here, and how often?"

I shoved aside my daze, continuing down the dark ally. The answers to his questions were at the back of my throat, but who was he to ask such things? Who was he to know my past? He wouldn't care anyway. He was only confused, and confusion made people believe that they wanted answers when really they didn't. The truth hurt. I wasn't about to deceive myself into thinking that he actually wanted to know.

Will followed me, exclaiming, "Sam, answer me!"

Spinning around, I was quickly face to face with him. I glared, but he only glared right back. I hated that I suddenly felt an urge to tell him everything though it would mean giving in. If he wanted the truth, I wasn't going to give him the satisfaction of the details.

Without breaking my stare, I said coolly, "I come out when I can. I come out here because this was my life, my home. I know them because I saved Elizabeth and Owen long ago. I don't wish to be called a princess because I'm not one, not really."

He looked at me quizzically. "How?"

"My real parents died when I was eight. I lived on the streets until I was twelve."

"What happened then?"

"I don't know," I nearly broke my whisper. "King Richard saw me save them. He saw something in me no one else did. He *saved* me."

Will studied me for some time, raising an eyebrow. "Really?"

I groaned. "I can prove it. See for yourself."

Turning around, I lifted up my shirt so that only my back was visible. Will's fingers slowly traced the scars from my whipping, leaving a tingling sensation I didn't feel at all comfortable with. I quickly pulled down my shirt and turned to face him again. "Do you believe me now?"

He nodded as if in a hazy confliction. My eyes searched his wandering green ones, not sure what ran around in his mind exactly. A brief thought that perhaps I should help detangle some of the confusion crossed my mind, but I didn't allow myself to give it any attention. Turning sharply around, I climbed up a building so as not to be caught on the streets. Will scurried up after me, but I didn't wait for him, continuing on my way to the castle in a steady silence.

Chapter Seven

After returning to the sleeping castle and falling into bed, Sam's words rang in my head over and over. I kept wondering how I couldn't have known that the Princess was adopted. Then again, how could I not know about that very same princess being a knight? Sam had said she'd been twelve when she was taken into the royal family, not in those words, but from what I deduced. I had only been a boy around that time, about fourteen. Being so young, I supposed I was never told. And then there were the scars! Those scars splitting her back, long and white. She would have never been whipped as a princess. Could that really be what she went through?

My gaze ventured out the window as the first peek of the sun came over the horizon. Its rays reached out over the village, bathing the streets with its glow. They flooded through the window and danced over my head, filling the room so that every crack and every corner was filled with the gift of light and warmth the sun bestowed.

A thump caused me to turn around to see John face down on the floor. Giving a groan, he sat up, his sleepy, displeased expression causing me to give a short laugh. John glared. "What did you do, sleep in your clothes?"

I looked down as I realized that I had not changed after Sam and I made it back to the castle. Shrugging, I gave a half-hearted smile. "Guess I was just really tired after that ball last night," I lied. I really didn't get much sleep at all last night, but when I managed to doze off, nightmares were waiting for me. They all featured Sam and each was more terrible and painful to watch than the last.

John grunted as he blinked at the light. "Well, I'm hungry. Better get ready for breakfast."

Getting up from breakfast, someone grabbed me by the arm. Resisting my instinct to instantly flip the person over, I instead whipped around to see who it was. My eyes narrowed slightly. Will. I clenched my jaw, still upset with him for last night.

"What do you want?" I asked, making sure the Queen was out of earshot.

Right now was not the time for a lecture about the mannerisms of a lady. I would hate for her to get any ideas as to what I would be doing out late at night with a knight, even if it was unintentional. I looked at Will's hand on my arm and then back up at his eyes. He got the hint and let go.

"I don't think we got off on the right foot," he started.

I cocked an eyebrow. "You think?"

Ignoring my statement, Will continued, "So, do you think we could just start over and be friends?"

"Friends?" Now I raised both my eyebrows.

"Yeah."

I pondered this for a moment. His request caught me off guard. A rejection was on the tip of my tongue, but the look in his eyes told me that his offer was genuine. I supposed he was right; we did start off on the wrong foot. I wondered if it would be any different between us if we hadn't, what with what happened last night. Maybe I shouldn't be so hard on him. He was obviously trying to make up for it. The least I could do was let him.

"Alright, look. The King and I are going hawking at noon. If you want," I sighed, "you could come and join us."

Will grinned. "I'll be there." He started to stride off, but quickly turned back around. "Thanks."

I smiled a little as he walked off, following everyone else. The room was now cleared, and the only ones who remained were the servants. One of them—Nancy, Elizabeth's cousin—came up behind me, her long brown hair tucked into a handkerchief around her head. I smiled at her and she shyly smiled back.

Clearing the table, I shook my head over the plates that still held scraps of food. When I lived on the streets, I would've thought such scraps to be a feast. I had seen men fight for such meager portions, kill for even less. Not a crumb would have been wasted. Here, food was so plentiful that people could afford not to finish their meal. How could there be such an abundance of food in some places and a famine in others? Such logic was strange to me, even now.

I supposed that it was because of my life on the streets that I helped with the servants sometimes. To me, it had never felt exactly right to be served the way royalty was supposed to be served. Especially when I was younger, I'd always had a yearning to learn as many useful talents as I possibly could. I managed to find at least a few servants who were willing to teach me when I was younger. Thank goodness for my curiosity, for otherwise I wouldn't be able to cook or heal or mend or even be a knight!

In return for their generosity, I helped out whenever I could. No one knew that I did so except for Millie, King Richard, and the servants, though I suspected that Queen Veronica had figured it out by now. So long as I continued to learn the duties of a princess and a lady, as well as those of a scholar—for the Queen was taught even book knowledge as a girl, though it was not so popular in her time— then I believed she was all right in my learning any other task I wished. Of course, as long as they fell under my morals as a Christian.

"Nancy," I said to break the uneasy silence, "when we're done clearing the table, will you tell me what else there is to do?"

"Of course, miss," Nancy responded softly, almost sadly.

I studied her as I put up plate after plate onto the cart, filling it up with the dirty dishes. No matter how hard she tried to hide it, I could tell she was upset. After all, I was experienced in reading other people's expressions and feelings. Sir Hugh and the King had taught me such during my training as a knight, and I picked up quite a few things like this on the streets. One must know if a man was so upset that he's willing to beat a child if one ran across the street before him. Or if a woman was in a heartfelt temper so as to spare a few morsels of food. Or if a dog was tame enough not to attack if one needed shelter for the night and one such canine already occupied the spot. Thus, it was easy for me to tell that Nancy was trying to hold back her tears.

"What's the matter?" I asked, still stacking dishes.

In a sudden burst of tears, Nancy sobbed out, "It's Garrick! He's hurt awfully bad! The doctor is out of town and won't be expected until next week. He may need stitches, but I can't handle blood. I'm afraid that without medical attention, he's going to lose his leg!" In hysterics, she collapsed into my arms and cried into my shoulder.

Garrick was Nancy's fiancé. A very nice and helpful man, he was a dear friend to me, joining the King and me whenever we went out on a hunt. He was the one who helped me with tracking. I eminently felt a since of urgency. "Where is he?"

Nancy pulled back, still sobbing. "In the cottage he's made for us once we're married. It's about two miles behind the stables."

I grabbed her by the shoulders and looked into her tear-filled eyes. "Nancy, I need you to listen to me very closely. Get a needle, thread, and whiskey as quickly as you can. You should be able to find the needle and thread in the sewing room. Talk to the cook about the whiskey; he'll know where it is. I'll meet you at the stables. Now go, and hurry!"

Nancy nodded and ran off. Quickly, I asked another servant—one who seemed the least shocked at hearing such news—to finish clearing the table and put the cart in the kitchen. Without waiting for a response from the woman without a kerchief, I turned and ran as fast as I could. I needed to get to the stables to saddle up Autumn, and quickly.

"What am I going to do, John?" I exclaimed in a panic.

"Why did you even accept the invitation? You don't know anything about falconry!" John acknowledged. "Well, at least I hope you know there's a bird involved."

"I don't know." I shrugged, ignoring the insult. "It was just something to have us start over, you know, be friends."

John cocked an eyebrow. "Friends?"

I threw my hands in the air and said in an exasperated tone, "Yes, friends! Is that so hard to believe?"

John shrugged. "Maybe you should cancel. You know, just say that you can't make it, that you forgot about some other plans you made before."

"It's the King! You can't just cancel on the King!"

"And Sam," John pointed out.

I sighed, "Yes, and Sam."

My mind raced, trying to find some way I could go and not embarrass myself. If only my father had taught me about falconry while he was still here. I remembered attending a few hawkings as a young boy. Father had only shown me the birds when they were put away where they were safely out of harm's way, but he never taught me the art of hunting with birds. By the time I was old enough to learn, he was already sick.

There had to be someone who knew how. Perhaps, someone in my party—those who had come with me to the castle from home. I believed some of my men used to go hawking with Father many years ago. Even if they were not experts, it would still be nice to have some insight before I went off with King Richard and the Princess.

I straightened my back as I made up my mind. "John, fetch me those who came with us. I must know who knows falconry, so they can teach me."

John stood up, a smile on his face, and stated, "Yes, sir." He laughed softly as he left to carry out my command.

I jumped off Autumn and burst through the door. Garrick was sprawled out on the bed. His blond hair was soaked with sweat, plastered to his forehead. His chest, heaving from pain, gasped for breath. Dark blood covered his left calf and shards of glass gleamed as the light fell over it.

I turned to Bertha, another servant who had been in the castle since before King Richard was crowned, when another much crueler king reigned. She knelt by Garrick's side, slowly pouring rye into his mouth for the pain. Garrick's whiskered chin was wet with the stuff.

"What happened?" I asked as I examined the wound.

Her usually rosy, but now pale, wrinkled face turned to me. "He went to pick up the window he ordered for this here cottage. He came back and when he was installing it, he fell and the glass shattered. There's lots of glass lodged inside." Her eyes shut briefly as she shuddered.

"Did you get the glass out?"

"I'm no doctor, dear. I can't handle a knife without causing more damage, and my eyesight isn't what it used to be, but I did manage to get some of the bigger pieces out," she explained as she gestured to a plate with bloody shards of glass on it. There weren't a lot, but at least she'd gotten some.

I nodded, reaching for my satchel as I instructed, "I need boiled water and some tweezers."

Bertha got up to fetch the supplies I asked for. Quickly, I brought out the things Nancy put in my satchel earlier. Using a nearby bowl, I poured some of the whiskey in it. After dropping in the thread to soak, I snatched a lighted candle from a table nearby. I held the needle over the small flame briefly before that too went in the bowl of whiskey. Setting these within reach, I used the rag that Bertha left to wipe away the blood, though I'm quicker and less merciful for speed. Garrick groaned pitifully. The bleeding wasn't as bad as I initially thought.

Bertha returned with another lighted candle and tweezers, saying that the water was heating. I took the tweezers eagerly and began, carefully pulling out the shards of glass I saw at first. My eyes searched frantically over his bloody foreleg, taking out any glass I found. Garrick kicked out in a reflex from the pain.

"You'll have to hold him down," I told Bertha in as calm a manner as I could manage.

She did so with difficulty, using her stout arms to keep Garrick from flailing so much. When my eyes finally swept over his calf for the fifth time without finding anymore glass, I put aside the tweezers. Blood began to flow again over the agitated skin. To keep Bertha holding him down, I rushed off to find the water set out to boil. Thankfully, the liquid was bubbling. Grasping the pot despite the heat, I made my way back to the barely conscious Garrick.

I let the water sit for a minute, allowing the bubbles to disappear and the steam to lessen. Taking the rag I used earlier, I soaked it in the hot water and washed the wound. Garrick cried out, wiggling again. Bertha had to practically lie on top of him to get him to hold still. I washed away the blood as well as a few glass splinters I missed before. Once the wound was as clean as possible, I set aside the bloody rag and removed the needle and thread from the whiskey. Once threaded, I bit my lip and ignored the tightening in my stomach. Bringing needle to skin, I began the painful and attention demanding task of stitching.

Garrick's screams rang in my ears, but I deafened myself to the noise. My hands stayed steady despite the lump in my throat, my demeanor calm and focused as it had to be in such situations. I hardly saw the blood anymore, just the stitches that my fingers did as if of their own accord. Thankfully, not much stitching was needed, for only the cuts made by the bigger shards of glass needed mending. Time passed quickly, seeming as if it had only been a few minutes when I put the needle aside. I took out the bandages in my satchel, the ones I always kept in it, and bound Garrick's calf.

Tying it off, I instructed Bertha, "Keep an eye on him until Nancy gets back. His bandages may need changing tomorrow, so you'll have to tell Nancy that too. If he shows any sign of a fever, let me know immediately." Hesitating briefly, I added, "You might want to give him more rye for the pain."

As I stood from my kneeling position, Bertha embraced me, squeezing tight. "Thank you, girlie. I'm starting to think I need to call you for all my problems. You sure are a hero."

I blushed. "I'm no hero. It was no problem, really."

"Well of course you're one!" Bertha exclaimed looking me dead in the eye. "Just look at all you've done. You're going to be a mighty fine queen someday, a mighty fine one indeed."

"Can I ask you something, Your Majesty?" I questioned hesitantly. I only just met him and who knew what the King was like exactly.

"If you wish," he responded, his voice deep.

I attempted not to get tongue tied. "When you were not yet king, and another ruled, how did you come about taking over Etheland?"

"Why, are you having ideas?" King Richard asked, raising a thick eyebrow with a chuckle.

"No, Your Majesty." I shook my head. "I was just curious. I loved to hear the stories as a boy, and I only wanted to hear what happened from the man himself."

"I see." The King nodded in understanding. "Well, son, the first thing you should know is that I had no real intentions of being king when I rebelled against Akelin."

"But, how...?" I started, but King Richard raised his hand to stop me.

"You wished to hear my story." He smiled. "Do you wish for me to tell it?"

I nodded, feeling as eager as I had as a boy when about to hear a great story. King Richard had been one of my childhood heroes. He still was, though I didn't obsess over him as I once did. The tales of his rising up to overpower the King Akelin flitted through my mind now, but I shoved them aside so as I had a fresh perspective for the real tale.

"I should begin by saying exactly why I rebelled against Akelin, for I assume you were not alive when he still reigned," he paused, waiting for my nod of agreement. "Akelin was not the kind of king who was easy to love. In fact, he used fear to control the people instead of admiration or kindness. He tore lives apart to prove a point: that none was to trifle with him. No one could say anything against him aloud, for Akelin had spies everywhere. Executions were a regular occurrence. Assassinations for no known reason were not uncommon. Houses that just happened to light aflame were a fact of everyday life. He raised taxes to impossible demands, took young men and older boys away to fight far off wars against lands such as Nonya and forced the families of so-called criminals to work in his mines. He took anything he wished. He tortured for entertainment. So cruel and heartless, the neighboring kingdoms of Tarn, Lynnia, Cileith, and even the countries of Farthend and Brisin feared to interfere with his affairs. Akelin left many children orphaned, many wives widowed, many parents childless, and everyone's hearts clouded with fear."

"Didn't anyone do something?" I asked without thinking.

"Most were too afraid to stand up to him, and those who did rebel ended up in the gallows, their families spontaneously killed," the King answered. "My parents were some of those who tried to stop the rein of Akelin. They began by starting a gathering of rebels, but when Akelin heard wind of it, he had my parents questioned, tortured, and finally murdered. I managed to escape the men who came to take me to the front lines of the battlefield. At that point, I had more hatred toward him than fear. I was sixteen."

He paused as if the memory were replaying before his eyes. His expression grave, his eyes had a far off look. I started to regret asking him about his story, for it obviously pained him to think about. Yet, he continued on anyway.

"After my parents died, I rose to leader of the rebellion. My father taught me something of fighting before he was gone and there were quite a few traitorous knights to Akelin in our uprising who were more than willing to teach me. Our group continued to grow as we rescued those on their way to the mines or to war, taking in escaped men and women who were falsely and truthfully called criminals," King Richard went on, his voice strained with passion. "I was hardly much older than you when our rebellion reached its peak. When we finally openly rose up against him, we found that plenty of his own soldiers switched forces, proving their disloyalty to their cruel ruler.

"I cannot explain exactly what happened during the fight, but I remember the blood. I remember the cold fear as if it were only yesterday. We lost so many lives in that battle, so many friends. War is not to be taken lightly, son. It should not be something desired. It should only come as a necessity, a last resort. To go to war is to bet with lives. That is not something one should do without taking each one into account. Even the bravest of us loath war, and those who long for it are the most dangerous. That was the kind of monster Akelin had been, and we defeated him."

My throat felt dry and tight. I always heard of the victory, the glory, the incredible battle that made Richard King. I never heard the dark side of it, never imagined the story as told by the King, as told by the men present at the time. It gave me more of a sad glimpse to the tale.

"Unfortunately, Akelin himself was not defeated," King Richard growled. "During the chaos he escaped, abandoning the men who still fought for him, the coward!"

"What happened to him?"

"Who knows," he responded. "He could have escaped to another country, started a new life under a new name. At least he's smart enough not to have shown his face in Etheland again. I believe that he's lying in an unmarked grave, his corpse rotting away and his soul locked up in hell."

I nodded, sure that his expectation was most likely true. "How did you become king?"

"The people insisted upon crowning me. A few of the knights who had turned against Akelin suggested finding his sister who had run away from the rein of her brother, but most believed her to be dead. Even if she were alive, the people were not willing to accept a relative of the wretched king to rise to the throne. Thus, I was made king," he smiled slightly, "and I certainly hope I've made a good one."

"You are the best king this kingdom has ever seen, Your Majesty," I insisted. "I wouldn't serve under any other."

"I'm glad to hear that, son." King Richard's stature brightened from the previous solemn state. "I'm glad to hear it. Now, enough of the sorrows and victories of my past. Let us enjoy in the sport of falconry. We'll wait for my daughter, of course, but at least we can get in better spirits and prepare for the hunt."

After a brief minute of debate, I decided to admit that I had never been hawking before. He seemed to understand after I explained that my father never taught me how. He allowed me to borrow one of the easier birds he owned, Grey, a peregrine falcon with a dark silver head and gray speckled feathers. A gentle, majestic creature, I remembered my father had owned a few peregrine falcons, and from what I recalled, they were fairly good hunters. Though, I was just a boy when I last saw them hunt, so I might have been mistaken. Grey's head was covered with a blue hood.

My attention was drawn from the King and his birds by a figure heading our way. A chestnut horse moving over the green hills at a rapid speed was carrying a red haired maiden on her back. As Sam pulled up beside the cart holding the King's hunting birds, I noticed how her shirt was stained with dark blood. Her face looked strained and relieved at the same time. What has Sam been doing?

"I apologize for being late. I was... busy," Sam explained as soon as she slipped off her mare and tethered her to a tree.

King Richard chuckled, "That's all right. Did the patient survive?"

Sam smiled. "Yes, he's much better now." An unspoken understanding between the two revealed itself in the twinkle of each other's eyes.

The King stroked his short, gray beard. Sam turned away, reaching into the cart holding the birds of prey. She brought out a cage covered with a deep brown tarp

69

embroidered with red-brown leaves. Sam removed the tarp to reveal a majestic Harris's Hawk, auburn as the earth with eyes of walnut. The beauty of this bird took my breath away.

Sam reached in and pulled a forest green hood over the hawk's eyes. After pulling on a thick glove, she opened the cage and brought out the bird perched on her gloved forearm.

"This," Sam spoke with proud admiration, "is Dawn."

I stroked Dawn's soft feathers. Her razor-like talons delicately perched on the thick glove covering my hand and lower arm. Her sharp, black tipped beak was slightly open, revealing her blue tongue. I always admired her beauty and free spirit. Her spirit was what we had most in common; neither of us could stay within an enclosed cage for long. I envied her ability to soar above the clouds. How I longed to breakaway and fly.

I turned to Will. "Who are you flying? Lightning? Bear?"

"Grey," Will answered.

"Grey. He's a gentle creature," I said. So, it's Grey. He was a sweet bird, but not the best hunter. Grey was also a beginner's hawk. I wondered...

King Richard cleared his throat. "Well, are we going to dilly dally, or hunt?"

I smiled at him. The King had always understood me. He was the one who first taught me how to use a sword before he found Sir Hugh to teach me such things. He gave me my first bow and arrows and made me one of the Great Knights. There was no way I could ever repay him for everything he's done, especially taking me in.

Will pulled on a thick glove and Grey hopped onto his arm. He had to adjust to the feel of the falcon's position. I laughed softly as the black speckled bird whacked Will repeatedly with his wings. King Richard chuckled at the sight of Will getting blow after blow in the face.

I laughed harder, "He likes you."

Will scowled. "Yeah, I'm feeling the love."

King Richard shook his head in amusement as he brought out his white and gray feathered gyrfalcon, Storm. The falcon's eyes were covered by a regal purple hood, the silver of his beak only just visible. When Grey finally calmed down, the King announced, "Get your birds ready, when I say so, take off the hoods. Ready? Go!"

With that, I whipped off the green hood immediately and Dawn was off! Her powerful wings took her higher and higher until she glided through open skies. I watched as she soared without a single flap of her wings, disappearing in and above the clouds. Grey took off, but he stayed just above the treetops, and Storm disappeared into the clouds behind Dawn. We all stared after the hawks as they vanished from sight.

I was the first to break the silence, "So, Will, this is your first time hawking, huh?"

Will looked at me, aghast. "How… how did you know?"

I smiled. "The way you held the bird was like you've never held a falcon before, which you haven't. Also, Grey is for beginners, not professionals."

"I should have known you'd catch on," King Richard chuckled. "You've always had a knack for noticing things."

Will hung his head in defeat as he officially admitted, "It's true. I never learned falconry."

I shrugged. "Well, better late than never."

The King's grin broadened and I caught a quick wink my way. "So Will, are you joining the archery competition tomorrow? If you win, you get a prize."

I gave a short laugh, "Yeah, *if* he wins."

Will ignored my comment. "I'll be there. Though, if you don't mind me asking, what sort of prize is it?"

King Richard's brown eyes turned my way. "A kiss, of course, from the Princess."

Will's eyebrows shot up in surprise as he looked to me. "You?"

"*If* someone wins," I exclaimed quickly, "and I'll see to it that that's impossible."

"Why? Will *you* be competing?" Will asked.

"Of course," I scoffed. "I'm not some prize to be won so easily."

"Well then," Will said, turning back to King Richard, "if *Sam* doesn't mind..."

"I'd like to see you try," I laughed.

Will smiled. "Then may the best archer win."

What was he thinking? I beat him at the joust far too easily. Now, he thought he could beat me at archery? My best weapon was a bow and arrow. I loved archery even more than sword fighting!

A falcon flew our way, Grey by the looks of it. Will held up his arm, but not the gloved one. Grey dropped his capture at Will's feet, then landed on his arm. Will gave a cry of pain as the talons sunk into his flesh, blood trickling down his arm. Grey, startled by the sudden cry, flapped his strong wings, causing his sharp talons to dig deeper into Will's arm. While he got continuous blows in the face and mouthfuls of feathers, King Richard and I rushed to his aid.

King Richard shouted above Grey's ear piercing screeches, "Sam, see to his arm. I'll take the bird."

I didn't respond to him; I just did what is necessary. Once King Richard pried the huge bird off Will's arm and moved to put the creature in his cage, I demanded to Will, "Give me your shirt!" He clutched his arm, as I shouted, "Now!"

Will quickly ripped off his shirt and I started tearing it to strips. Pressing my hands hard against the deep talon piercings, I gave him the strips of shirt, remembering the whiskey in my satchel. I told him to continue to apply pressure to the puncture wounds while I ran for the bag I put in the cart earlier. Grabbing the bottle, I rushed to Will's side and poured the liquid on all eight punctures. Will gasped in pain, but still I poured until the bottle was empty. Taking the strips, I began wrapping his arm, making a bandage.

"There," I stated.

Will smiled weakly at me. I gave a little smile back. The King seemed to have gotten Grey under control and back in his cage. I wasn't surprised, seeing as all birds seemed to love him.

King Richard said, "Did I forget to mention, Grey might be a *little* afraid of loud noises."

Will managed a small laugh, "Yeah, I can tell. Thank you." He looked down at his feet. "Hey, my first catch!" He held up the small mouse Grey had caught with a wry smile. We all start laughing heartily.

I heard a screech and looked up to see a white streak drop a hare at King Richard's feet, circle, and come to land on his master's outstretched arm, the gloved arm that is. King Richard gave Storm a piece of meat as he stroked his beloved bird.

I shaded my eyes in search for Dawn.

"Where's your hawk?" Will asked.

"She'll be here when she's ready. Where's your shirt?" I asked playfully.

Will looked down at his bare chest, pointing to his bandaged arm. "Right here."

"Sam raised her hawk since it was able to fly. She's trained Dawn well," King Richard said with pride.

I smiled at the memory of the tiny Harris's Hawk. No one thought Dawn would be much of a hunter because she was so small, except for me. I trained and raised her to be a great hunter in the King's mew. The smaller than average bird of prey had proven all those who ever doubted her wrong.

Will started to say something, but I held up a finger to quiet him, never taking my eyes off the sky. Suddenly, a screech pierced the quiet. Dawn soared through the air and dropped a small wild turkey on the ground in front of me. She landed gracefully on my outstretched gloved arm, her brown eyes twinkling with pride. I smiled as I fed Dawn a piece of raw meat.

"A fine catch," the King complimented.

"Sure, turkey is a nice capture," Will grinned, "but I'd like to see you get a rat like mine!"

We all laughed hysterically as we prepared our birds for another venture. This time, Will put gloves on both arms. I shook my head and smiled to myself. Maybe the friendship thing between us wouldn't be so bad after all.

Chapter Eight

"So if you win… you get a kiss?" John asked.

"Yes."

"From Sam?"

"Yes."

"The one you're trying to be friends with?"

"Ye-" I stopped. I hadn't thought of that. But then again, I might not win.

As if John read my mind, he said, "You're like a champion at archery! There is a really big chance that you *will* win."

That was true. I was stringing a bow before I could even lift up a sword, or my mother used to say so, at least. She used to boast about me a lot, though it embarrassed me every time she did so. But now, I missed even her most embarrassing retellings. What I wouldn't give to have her support and love again. What I wouldn't give to have her *here* again, her advice being much appreciated at the moment.

"Well, I told the King himself that I would be there," I said mostly to myself rather than to John. "And Sam *did* say that she'd like to see me try."

John sighed, "Then I guess you'll need to get prepared for tomorrow."

I nodded, still trying to convince myself that it's a good idea. Grabbing my bow and quiver full of arrows, I headed out the door.

Millie barged through the door. "Why aren't you ready?"

"I am ready. Am I going to sit around and act all pretty with a sure chance of some total stranger stealing my kiss? Not if I can help it! I'm going to compete and, hopefully, keep my kiss," I explained.

The contest was King Richard's idea, but Queen Veronica insisted that the prize be my kiss. Of course King Richard agreed, though reluctantly. I suspected this was another attempt to find a suitor for me. I should've known better than to expect the Queen to give up so easily, but she wasn't anticipating me to put up a fight. I hated to oppose her so openly, but my heart and who I gave it to was my business. I told her so a thousand times before, but I believed she was getting desperate seeing as I was twenty-one and have never been in any romantic relationship. I knew that Queen Veronica had the best intentions, though I didn't always know exactly what they were. Still, my heart was my business. She was in for a big surprise.

Millie nodded in understanding. "I should have known that you would find *some* way out of it sooner or later! How silly of me."

I smiled. "You're always silly, Millie."

She gave a joyful giggle, "You rhymed! Get it? Silly and Millie!"

I laughed at her comment. Sometimes, Millie could act much younger than she really was. It was nothing to be ashamed of. Having the ability to see the light in everything was an excellent trait to have. There was always room in life to smile and laugh.

"*So*," Millie asked, changing the subject, "how did yesterday's hawking go?"

"It went great! Will was a little rusty on falconry, but he got some good game," I replied with a laugh. "I really think we could be friends. Though, he did get... punctured."

Millie's eyes widened. "What did you *do* to him?"

"It wasn't me, honest." I threw my hands up in defense. "He did it to himself! Well, technically Grey did..."

Millie placed her hands on her hips. "Then I wish you best of luck at the archery tournament."

With that, she took her leave. I didn't think she believed me. She had heard of incidents with other men that had occurred on my watch, though most had been accidents. I would probably not believe myself if I hadn't been on the scene. I patted my dog on the head before grabbing my bow and quiver full of arrows and headed on to the archery contest.

There must've been about thirty other competitors waiting for their turn at the archery contest. I searched the group for any sign of red hair. I couldn't find Sam. The only red haired competitor was a huge man with a scruffy beard, his look seeming to be foreign and his accent confirming his long travel from Brisin.

I scanned the audience in case Sam was forced not to compete. Her friend was there, the blonde one, but I didn't see Sam with her. I saw the Queen, though, beside the King. She had a bright, triumphant smile on her face. Wait, never mind! Her smile quickly vanished and her face fell slightly. I followed her gaze.

A hooded figure stalked to the back of the line of competitors. If it were not for the slight reveal of long red hair underneath the shaded hood I wouldn't have recognized Sam. Undoubtedly, it was her. Being in the center of the line, I believed she wanted to go against the one who beat everyone else, so she could keep her kiss. Last in line was certainly an advantage, I supposed.

I watched as man after man competed against the other, trying to be the closest to the center of the target. The crowd cheered and scoffed, growing louder as the competition narrowed down.

Finally, it was my turn. My competitor was a big, burly man from Lynnia with hard eyes and a greedy smile. I took my place in front of the target, waiting for the Lynnian to make his mark. He was too confident, too sure of himself, his cockiness causing him to make a risky move. Quickly, too quickly, he released his arrow, just inches away from the center. The Lynnian gave me a crude smile filled with a daring challenge without any words escaping his lips.

I stepped up, set an arrow and drew back the string. I took a deep breath, letting myself get calm enough to aim properly. As I let it out, I released with a twang. A cheer broke through the crowd as my arrow met the target dead in the center.

Look at them, thinking they could just go ahead and kiss me! It was repulsing! Most of these men were either twice or half my age. Surprisingly, there were many foreigners—probably traders due to the time of year. Just wait until I got out there. I'd show them that my heart and my kiss would not be taken so easily.

Queen Veronica didn't look pleased though she didn't seem surprised either. I almost wondered how she recognized me from such a distance and with me wearing my cloak, but I supposed all mothers recognized their children—adopted or not—despite having a hood covering their heads. I felt bad for opposing her, but not enough to step out of the arena. She couldn't do anything to stop me without stopping the archery contest, and she couldn't just stop an archery contest because a girl wanted to keep her kiss.

Will beat competitor after competitor. It just went to show how many men signed up who had little to no experience with a bow. He didn't even miss the center! He was better than I thought. I may have some serious competition here. I *definitely* underestimated him.

Now, it was Will against the last man before me. Will released his arrow, again making a perfect shot. The other man—more of a boy than a man—released his arrow. His posture was shaky, causing the arrow to miss the target all together. The crowd roars. As I stepped up, I let my hood fall back and everyone went quiet. The reaction was not surprising; it had happened several times before.

I nodded to my competitor. "Will."

He nodded back. "Sam."

"How's your arm?"

Will looked down at his bandaged forearm. "It's a little better now."

"Good to hear. Good luck to you."

"And to you."

I gestured to the target in front of him, indicating for him to go first. Will started, and again his arrow met the center. He looked back at me and gestured to my target. I held up my bow and fitted an arrow on the bow string. Taking a deep breath, I drew it back only to let it fly, piercing the very center of the target.

Gasps and chatter went through the crowd. The targets were moved back, and then a hush followed once more. Will smiled at me before his arrow went by with a twang, right in the middle of the target. I gave him a slight, short smile before I too released my arrow into its destination: dead center. A wave of whispering flowed over the audience, and again a sudden quiet as the targets were moved back a second time.

I knew that if we both made this shot it would be a draw. I secretly hoped a sudden gust of wind would blow Will's arrow off course.

This time, I went first. I set up my bow and fitted the arrow, drawing it back so that the feathered end brushed my cheek. I found I was holding my breath, so I let it out right before I let the arrow soar. I watched as it whistled through the air and entered the exact middle of the target.

I smiled and watched as Will readied his arrow. I could tell he was nervous, but he covered it well. He drew back his arrow and a gasp spread throughout the crowd, followed by a series of whispers as Will's arrow sunk into the heart of the target. It was a draw!

"Well, I suppose since none of us won, then neither of us gets the prize." I shrugged.

Will gave a twitch of a smile. "If that's what you wish."

The shock at his reply made my chest pressurize. I knew that the prize went to whoever won, and seeing that Will won as well as I, he technically had the right to claim my kiss. He should have demanded his prize. Shouldn't he? Any other man here would have. I heard their boasts, read their expectant faces. So why wouldn't he? The answer came to my mind before the question had fully been pondered. Will was not any other man.

Gossip-filled murmur went through the crowd. I turned to see the Queen entering the arena. Her face had a fixed expression of determination. I knew what she had to say before the words came out of her mouth, "It was *royal decree* that whoever won would get a kiss from the Princess. Since Sir William has won, he shall get his reward."

My eyes searched the Queen's face, wondering why she was suddenly so stubborn with this. A flicker of an apology seemed to glaze over her eyes. Her statement replayed in my mind and the annunciation of two words made sense to me now. *Royal decree*, an official statement that fixed the prize. If I were to rebel against such, it would suggest severe disrespect toward the King and Queen. It was testy enough being the adopted princess and a knighted woman. If any of the neighboring kingdoms heard of such a disagreement to a *royal decree* then it could cause problems to King Richard and to Etheland.

Queen Veronica stepped closer, speaking softly enough for only Will and me to hear, "I apologize, but it must be done."

"I understand," I whispered, receiving a thankful smile from the Queen.

Will, seeming to also understand the situation, nodded in comprehension. He stepped closer to me, but my feet felt frozen to the ground. My stomach twisted in knots and my throat closed tight. Will was so near now that I felt his breath on my skin, the closeness making me uncomfortable. He put his hand on my neck, pressing his forehead to mine. My eyes cast down, afraid to look into his.

"Are you sure about this?" Will whispered so softly I could hardly hear him.

I nodded slightly, telling myself over and over that it was for King Richard, it was for Queen Veronica. I caught a quick glimpse of his eyes before he pressed his lips to mine. The kiss wasn't long, though it seemed as if it stretched on for endless time. It took a few more seconds before Will pulled away completely.

My ears buzzing, I was only vaguely aware of the crowd's reaction. I was glad for my unfocused senses; for otherwise I was sure I would be all the more uncomfortable. Will disappeared before I could focus on his reaction, and as my eyes searched the sudden crowd, the Queen placed a hand on my arm and led me away. She didn't say anything, and I was glad for it. My mind was too much of a confused mess to make sense of anything at the moment.

Chapter Nine

Even after a whole day of hazy pondering, I still couldn't get yesterday's event out of my head. I almost wished I had stayed longer, just to see Sam's further reaction, but I was afraid of what that would have been exactly. I still was. Was she angry, frustrated? Did she hate me now? Perhaps I shouldn't have joined the contest at all. That could have meant that Sam would have to kiss someone else. Strangely, I hated that thought even more than I felt guilty of winning the archery contest, even if it was a draw. If I had let Sam win completely, would things have gone differently yesterday? I didn't think so.

What now? I tried so hard for us to be friends; now I was afraid I'd ruined it all. Did she hate me? The thought made my chest hurt. I didn't think I could stand that. I had to find out. I couldn't fool myself into assuming what Sam was thinking when I hadn't the slightest idea. She could hate me, but then again, she might not. Avoiding her wasn't going to make things easier. Better to confront it now than face years of regret.

My mind made up, I headed out to find her.

Turning around the corner, I found myself suddenly on the floor. Again. Shaking my hair out of my face, I recognized Will instantly.

"Must every time I turn this corner, you somehow end up on top of me," I said, rolling out from underneath him. Once on my feet, I held out my hand to him. He took it, and I hoisted him up.

"Sorry… again," Will apologized.

"No problem. I'm starting to think this really is Crash Corner." I shrugged it off.

"Yeah, seriously."

I studied Will for some time. "What's wrong?"

"I just, I wasn't sure how you would react seeing me," Will struggled to get the words out. "With what happened yesterday, I thought…"

I stopped him. "It's not your fault. It was a royal decree, and it would have caused a problem if you didn't… you know. It doesn't mean I hate you. We're still friends—if you wish it."

Will sighed in relief. "Yes, I'd like that."

I put my hand on his shoulder. "If it makes you feel better, I'm going riding. Come with me if you want. It's been a while since I've had a companion. Wait, you do know how to ride a horse, *right*?" I teased.

Will laughed, "*Yes*, I know how to ride a horse, and I'd enjoy that. I could use fresh air."

I smiled. "Alright. I'm sure it will be fun." Despite this new and strange sensation in my gut, I meant it.

"Yahoo!" Sam whooped.

I laughed. Her hair was blown back so as it seemed like actual flames. My paint-horse, Billy, and Sam's mare were in a gallop down a path through the trees that made up the forest. The wind in my face and the speed of our horses were exhilarating! A doe leapt away, followed by her spotted fawn. The birds soared away overhead. Rabbits hopped out of the way so they wouldn't be trampled under the horses' powerful hooves.

I didn't know where Sam was leading me. I wondered if she knew either. We'd been riding for quite a while, far out of the town, but I had not a care in the world for such matters. My enjoyment was too high.

Suddenly, a branch hit me square in the face, resulting in me getting a mouth full of leaves and a smarting nose! Sam looked back and laughed while I spit out the nasty plants.

We went on for some time until we entered a clearing. Sam suddenly stopped Autumn in her tracks, so I halted Billy as well. I noted our surroundings: an old well, and then nothing but the vast, open land. There seemed to be some kind of mound of blackened stone shapes and burnt, rotting wood on the edge of the clearing. My mind registered it to be the skeleton of a house, though a diminished one at that.

Looking over at Sam, her face seemed as if she was trapped in a haunted memory.

"Sam," I asked, "Sam, are you all right?"

I got no response from her. Her eyes were glassy and filled with tears that wouldn't spill.

"Sam?" I asked again.

She slipped off her horse and sunk to her knees. Her position turned towards the house remnants, never taking her eyes from it.

"Sam!"

Will repeated my name over and over, but the words only brushed past my ears. Even now, I felt the heat of the flames again, burning my skin. The screams rang in my ears, my own screams and... *theirs*. Smoke seemed to fill my lungs, the roaring flames eating away at wood... and flesh.

I awakened from my horrid flashback by a hand on my shoulder. That was when my ears caught the word Will said once more, "Sam?" Looking up at him, his green eyes overflowed with concern and confusion.

"I didn't realize I was leading us here. We shouldn't have come," I whispered under my breath.

Will sat down in front of me on the yellow grass and stared at me with a question in his face, a question that was so painful to answer, but one that could not be ignored. Taking out the chain around my neck, I fingered my mother's ring. I looked with eyes that were blind to the present, but vivid in seeing the past. My breath was painful as I relived the most tragic time of my life.

"I was eight. I had gone to get the water from our well as I did every morning. There were more trees then, between

the well and the house. Otherwise I would have seen it…"
My voice trailed off.

Will grabbed my trembling hand and encouraged me to
keep going. I took another deep breath and continued, "I was
coming back to my house with the buckets. That's when I
smelled the smoke and saw the flames rising higher and
higher. My house, my home, was ablaze with a fire that
could not be extinguished easily. Without thinking, I ran
inside. In the midst of the flames my father was helping
support my mother, who was injured by a wall that had
fallen on her leg. She thrust my baby sister Hanna into my
arms and told me to get her out of there. She said that they
would be right behind me. I made it out, but as I did a fire-
ridden wall collapsed on top of my parents." A tear slipped
down my cheek. "Hanna and I escaped, but my parents…
they didn't make it." More tears escaped my eyes.

Will pondered a moment. "What happened to her, your
sister I mean?"

"I gave her to a close friend of my parents." I continued
to finger my mother's ring. "I couldn't stay. They were poor,
couldn't take in two more mouths to feed. Hanna wasn't old
enough to remember anything. Hopefully she could live a
non-scarred, normal life."

"A normal life," Will said under his breath.

I managed to give a short laugh through my tears,
"Yeah. If you hadn't noticed, I'm not exactly *normal*."

"What started the fire?"

I pondered a moment. "I don't know. No one ever
figured that out."

"And the ring?" Will pointed to the golden ring hanging
around my neck that I was still clinging on to.

"It was my mother's, my *real* mother that is," I responded, studying the emerald embedded in the object I rubbed. "Hanna has one exactly like it, the same intertwining golden vines wrapped around the precious gem, except hers is a ruby, not an emerald. My mother used to say that the vines were like the two of us, Hanna and me, and that we are intertwined with each other so that there was no separating us. I just wish it were like that now." I took a deep breath. "Since that day when... it happened, I've been terrified of fire. My whole life turned upside down because of those red hot flames."

I noticed Will still holding my hand. The strange feeling in the pit of my stomach returned again. Despite the comfort brought with the touch, I took it away and quickly wiped away my tears.

"I'm sorry," he whispered.

"No, don't apologize," I said. "We should probably be heading back now."

I stood up and easily swung onto Autumn's back. I shook away, or at least hid my sadness and mustered a smile. "Race you back!"

As Autumn fell into a gallop, I heard Will shout, "Hey! That's not fair!"

I only laughed in response.

Chapter Ten

The white kerchief still lay beside my bed, a reminder of the puzzling tail on my second day at the castle. Picking it up, I ran a thumb over the fabric, only now noticing the faded stains that tainted the color. I resolved to leave the mystery unsolved and stuffed the kerchief in my pocket.

I had only just seen to the last bit of packing. Today was the day my party and I left the King's castle to return home. Home. It seemed so strange saying it. It was the place I lived, the territory I looked over, the people I cared for—but home did not seem the right word for it. It hadn't quite been home for years. Not like it used to be.

I took one last look at the room I occupied for the past few weeks. Time had gone by so fast since we came for the jousting tournament. I enjoyed it here and I looked forward to our next meeting with the King and his family. I especially looked forward to seeing Sam again. With a finalized sigh, I slowly close the door behind me.

Will was leaving. I wasn't sure how I felt about that. Of course, I was saddened, for he seemed to have become quite a good friend, but there was something else. I was outside with King Richard and Queen Veronica to bid him farewell. I smiled at him, receiving a smile back.

King Richard clapped Will on the back heartily, saying, "It was wonderful to meet you, William. I do hope to see you soon. You are welcome here anytime." He gave Will a wide grin.

Will bowed his head, smiling. "Thank you, Your Majesty."

King Richard chuckled. Queen Veronica held out her hand, and Will pressed a quick kiss on the back of her bejeweled fingers. I rolled my eyes and stifled back a laugh. The Queen could be so formal in her ways. It was impressive at times, but to me, it could get to be a bit much.

Will turned to me, inclining his head. I did the same, for this time, I was required to be at least a little formal.

Will's eyes twinkled. "Don't forget, we still have some unfinished business about that race."

I laughed, "Autumn and I beat you fair and square, yesterday!"

"You won because you got a head start." Will grinned. "Good-bye, Sam."

"No, not good-bye," I insisted, taking his hand, "until next time."

Will squeezed my fingers before letting go to hoist himself up onto Billy's back.

Something caught my eye and the hairs on the back of my neck rose. I turned to face the hills, rolling into one another like waves in the sea, ending at the edge of the forest. Over one of these hills rode a messenger on a pony. By the speed he was riding, the pony must been weary. Why wouldn't he ride a faster horse?

The messenger rode up to King Richard, nearly falling off the old pony's back as the beast herself trembled on weary knees. The messenger wheezed, his wide eyes crazed, "We've been attacked."

I slid off my horse, waiting for the messenger to catch his breath to explain what happened. Sam rushed to the man's side. "What is—?"

The messenger grasped her shoulder, turning toward her, his voice heavy and shaky, "They are coming… Help them."

Dropping to his knees again, the man's face was hidden from view. Long, gray hair hung over his face in sweat soaked strands. I followed Sam's gaze beyond the hills. A thin, dark line traced the horizon, barely visible, but not unrecognizable: people.

Sam took immediate action, grabbing the closest servant and telling her to get more people to help. Everything was soon a bustle of chaos; especially upon the distinguishable sight of the first figure of many appear in the distance. The King also took matters into his own hands.

"I need men to get horses and wagons," he ordered to a random assortment of servants. "Tell them to get those people as soon as possible."

"And when they get here, check for injuries," Sam added. "For cuts, clean with whiskey and bandage it if necessary. If they need stitches, get the physician. Tell him I sent for him. If they have bruises, be gentle and check for broken bones; the physician will know what to do. Burns, I have a special cream in the healing room that you can put on them. Anything else, get the physician or myself."

Taking action myself, I turned to my squire. "John, you and the men see to it that the King's orders are carried out. Wagons and horses, got it?"

John nodded, stunned and obviously confused.

"When that's done, be sure to follow Sam's instructions," I added. "I have a feeling the servants will need all the help they can get."

The King stooped down to the messenger kneeling on the floor in exhaustion. "Get up, man! Where are you from?"

His voice heavy with fatigue, the man answered, "The house… of Sir William…"

My heart stopped, my breath frozen. Terror seeped through my skin. My house? The place that was attacked was mine? That meant that the people headed ever so slowly this way were my people! How could this have happened?

The King's eyes turned to me, his expression grim. "William, come with me."

I nodded, following him in a haze. The messenger stood with a struggle, and I managed to snap out of my stupor to help him. Seeing his face full on for the first time since his arrival, my heart gave a leap as I recognized the man I had entrusted to watch over things while I was gone. Levi was an old family friend, a retired knight who had been very close to my father. I couldn't believe I didn't recognize him before!

"William," Levi whispered my name repetitively in shaky exhales of breath, "William."

"Samantha, Veronica," King Richard called, "you come, too. We need to go somewhere private. Now."

We entered the library in haste, for this was the only room where we could find solitude, closing the doors behind us. The King ordered a servant that we were not to be disturbed. As we all were seated, I quickly turned my eyes to Will. His face was grave, eyes focused on nothing but the old messenger. Obviously, he wanted to find out who attacked his people, probably more than the rest of us.

King Richard encouraged the messenger to begin. Taking a deep breath, the man commenced his story in full, "We've come from the house of Sir William of the Silver Blade. It was the day after William should have arrived at the castle of King Richard for the jousting tournament. We did not expect the attack..." His voice trailed off.

"Who? Who is responsible for putting this attack upon you?" King Richard questioned.

The messenger looked in the King's direction, but it was as if he was *looking* but not *seeing*, as if he was seeing a distant memory, a nightmare. His eyes filled with terror and his voice shook, "Akelin. He has returned."

Queen Veronica gasped and King Richard's grip on the arms of his chair tightened so much I could see the veins in his knuckles. Fear crawled into the library, gripping the hearts of everyone in the room. I felt its boney, cold fingers clutch my own heart. I saw Fear's cruel smile, almost hearing the terrified screams that followed it wherever it went. It sent an icy shudder down my spine.

Akelin was once the king of this land, penetrating his best friend and weapon, Fear, into the hearts of many. Before I joined the royal family, before I was even born, he was the cruelest of rulers Etheland had ever known, using his faithful servant, Fear, to control the people. Today, even his name brought Fear into the most courageous of hearts. Akelin disappeared after King Richard defeated his army; no one had heard of him since. Now, he was back?

"But, how can you be sure?" Queen Veronica spoke up, her voice quavering slightly. "They might only be a new mob of criminals. How can you be certain it is Akelin?"

The messenger stayed silent as if hesitant to respond. Slowly, he pulled a bundle out of his coat pocket, a fabric of some kind. The color was dark. That was all I could say of the package, for I only got but a quick look before a reaction I had not expected came from the King.

"Put that away," King Richard ordered, his tone foreboding. "Do not show it to anyone until we hold a gathering."

The man nodded, concealing the bundle again. The messenger's stature was still terrified, his beard quaking with his chin, his fingers flying to his mouth. It was as if he was trying to hold back a cry of fright.

I broke the silence, "What happened?"

The messenger turned to me. "They came in the dead of night. The hooves of their horses like thunder, the flash of their blades, lightning. They bore the crest of Akelin, the Screaming Skull. We barely escaped though I think they wanted us to make it out to tell the tale. They took the food and precious possessions, destroying anything that wasn't of use to them. They took up the children, causing havoc, only to put them outside the town gates. Once almost everyone was out, they lit the houses on fire! They took the horses, except the old pony, for she's not of much use for fast riders. The people still inside when the flames arose managed to escape, but were badly burned. Akelin's piercing, victorious cry rang through the sky." Turning directly to Will, he said, "The house of Sir William of the Silver Blade... is no more."

A deathly silence filled the room. I couldn't even hear myself breathe or my heart beat. The world itself seemed to have stopped and time froze. I knew that the same thought raced through all of our minds: *Akelin had returned; Akelin had returned; Akelin had returned!*

Chapter Eleven

The King sent messengers to all of the Great Knights to gather at the Golden Rose, a protected house, to discuss the return of Akelin and figure out what to do. I was to ride there with him, Sam, and Levi, which was why I was repacking. While the King's gone, Queen Veronica would take care of Etheland, but in secret. No one could know that the King was to leave the castle, besides some such as me. Otherwise, people would wonder where he went, rousing suspicion. We could not risk news of the King's absence reaching the ears of the enemy.

My mind ventured to my people. They arrived at the castle shortly after we heard what Levi had to say, thanks to the horses and wagons sent for them. Many of the people had burns on their hands, arms, legs, and even their faces! The clothes on their backs were singed and burnt, their hair tipped black and covered in ash. My heart gave a jolt as I remembered the state of those I was given the responsibility to look after.

Sam and I helped with tending them. We applied a special cream on the burns of those who had been licked by the flames. Servants brought out food and water for the people, who fell upon it like animals, so hungry they were. Some of the servants even cut hair for them to get rid of the singed parts. John and I showed the men where to wash, as Sam did for the women and children. All was well for my people, or at least as well as it could be for now.

As I continued to pack, I tried—though not successfully—not to think about the return of Akelin.

It was the dead of night when even the hunting creatures were silent. We rode for the Golden Rose—Will, King Richard, some other soldiers, and I. We were cloaked and hooded so as to remain undercover, lessening our chances of being seen and recognized. I had my sheathed sword at my waist and my bow and quiver full of arrows placed over my shoulders like a sash, ready to attack if the need arose.

We traveled through the woods so it would be less of a chance of our being discovered. Knights were trained to know how to get to the safe house, the Golden Rose, blindfolded. King Richard established it after he was made king, although, I had never ventured there for of the reasons it was made. This would be my first gathering of the Great Knights.

The moon was barely visible through the tree branches looming over head. I heard the swift rush of the river somewhere nearby. We had to be close. Following the river, we came upon a two-story house: the Golden Rose.

I slipped off Autumn and led her to the stables as did the others. After getting her situated, I walked up to the stonewalled doorway and entered the Golden Rose. Will was already inside, his face grim and thoughtful.

"What is it?" I asked.

"I just have this feeling…" his voice trailed off.

"What?" I asked again.

A faint noise came from the ceiling, interrupting my train of thought. *Pat, pat, pat.* Footsteps. I slowly grasped my bow and pull it off my shoulder.

Will looked back at me as he whispered, "We're not alone."

The door opened behind us and King Richard stepped through. I put a finger to my lips to indicate to keep quiet. He nodded in understanding as he heard the footsteps upstairs. He and I drew our swords slowly and Sam fitted an arrow in her bow. She pulled it back, ready to release it if the need arose.

Step after step came closer. A faint light from around the corner became brighter as the source neared. The steps grew louder. A hand holding a lantern came around the corner, the man to which the hand belonged making an appearance. He held up the lantern, revealing his face.

Sam lowered her bow slightly. "Sir Edrick."

Sir Edrick looked with sleepy eyes at Sam. "Hello, Princess."

Her grip tightened around her bow, knuckles whitening. With her jaw clenched and eyes lit as such, I was almost afraid Sir Edrick was about to get an arrow in the throat, but Sam lowered the bow to her side, placing the arrow back in her quiver. Remembering the cold edge of her knife when last I called her Princess, my free hand instinctively touched my throat. Sam's pale eyes glanced my way, probably recalling the same memory. Of course, the corner of her mouth twitched in a smirk.

Sir Edrick turned to the King, who already sheathed his sword. "Your Majesty," the knight greeted, bowing.

King Richard responded, "Edrick, we thought you were an intruder."

"I see," Edrick said, eyeing the sword I still held out in front of me. I sheathed it. Sir Edrick extended his hand. "Sir Edrick the Knife Bearer, but feel free to call me Edrick."

I shook his hand and introduced, "Sir William of the Silver Blade." Assessing whether to respond with familiarity—as Edrick had done—or formality, I decided to add, "I go by Will."

Edrick was one of the more famous knights. He gained his territory after his uncle died and he became the youngest man to be a Great Knight. He won his title, the Knife Bearer, for his uncanny skills with a dagger, and he was rumored to have killed thirty enemy invaders with only a short blade. About twenty-six years old now, he was a little taller than me with blond hair that fell over his shoulders and brown eyes. It appeared that he must have been going to sleep before he came down, for he wore his nightshirt.

King Richard spoke up, "We shall gather when Sir Hugh arrives. Until then, you're free to rest. I'll send for you when he gets here."

Sam nodded, turning toward her bedroom. Edrick led me to the room we shared with all the other knights and the King went off to his own chambers.

Lying on a small straw bed, I drifted off to sleep just as the colors of dawn appeared in the sky.

Chapter Twelve

"We should attack!" Sir Hugh exclaimed as he pounded his fist on the table.

"We haven't the slightest idea if Akelin truly is back," Edrick pointed out. "It could be impersonators who attacked Will's residence, a disguised threat."

The messenger, whose name I only recently discovered as Sir Levi, an old knight of King Richard's army, looked up gravely from where he was seated. His condition was better, though not by much, since his arrival yesterday at the castle. Dark eyes, tired under his thick brows as if he hadn't slept for days, still held a haunted look in them. The lines on his face were deep and sullen, adding ten years to his appearance. The glare he cast fixed upon Edrick held a silent fury coupled with fear.

Reaching into the folds of his cloak, Levi pulled out a lump of fabric, the color black as night. I recognized the bundle from the day before when he told us his tale in the library. With shaking fingers, he unfolded the material, the cloth growing larger and larger. Standing, the old knight threw the fabric over the table to reveal the full expanse of the flag. At the sight of it, an eerie silence befell over the Great Knights around the table.

"A disguised threat, you say," Sir Levi's voice was heavy, his accent broken slightly. "The flag of Akelin is a relic only the man himself owned. Only one was ever made; only one was ever used," his finger pressed against the center of the flag where it bore the Screaming Skull, Akelin's emblem, "and yet here it lies."

I knew the tales of Akelin and his flag. My father, my real one, used to tell me all sorts of stories when I was little, Akelin almost always used as the villain. The legend of his flag was one that was not entirely fictional, and everyone knew of it. The flag was the only one ever crafted. Some said it was embroidered with the hairs of his victims. Others said that the dyes used were made with tears instead of water. Still more said that the fabric itself was woven by the devil himself.

Yet the flag before me held no spectacular or demon qualities. The fabric was rich, to be sure, though weathered from all the battles it had seen. The emblem was terrifying, but was no different from any other item that bore Akelin's crest. This made the flag all the more horrifying. To think such an ordinary thing could exude so much meaning, so much power, was a nightmare in itself. All the history and the blood spilled under this flag's shadow seemed to hold a dark and sinister aura around it.

Taking the folds of fabric in his hands, King Richard flung the accursed thing aside. It landed in a pile on the floor, left there to prove its place in this house.

"So it is true then," Hugh exclaimed, his passion never leaving him. "This only encourages our need to attack!"

"We don't even know where Akelin's troops are, nor how many he has gathered," Will protested. "How are we to attack?"

"You run your sword straight through 'em, *that's* how," Sir Hugh slurred.

"I think the great Sir Hugh has had a little too much to drink," Sir Edrick laughed as if the tension were not thick enough in the air.

Sir Hugh scowled at him and yelled, "Even if I *did* have too much drink, I'd still have a better mind than *you*!"

"Please, let us not be irrational. Sir Hugh, put away that bottle before you do something stupid," I reasoned.

Edrick winked at me, a smirk on his face that made me shift uncomfortably. Sir Hugh looked at the bottle in his hand, seemingly ready to be smashed over Edrick's head. He muttered a few words as he set the glass on the table and settled down.

Hugh was a short, round man with a long, thick brown beard. He looked more like a dwarf in one of the fairytales Father used to tell me when I was a young child. He even had the attitude of one. Still, I was grateful to him for all he had done in my life. He was, after all, the one who trained me. Hugh was like an uncle to me, even if his temper could get the best of him. At least he was willing to accept a woman into the circle of the Great Knights straight away. Shaking my head, I brought myself back to the present.

The afternoon sun shone through the small window down over the map on the table. Little flags were scattered over its surface, though some were knocked over from the fabric previously laid over it. I stood on the right side of the King and Sir Hugh was on the left. Sir Edrick was next to him and Will next to me, Levi sitting on the other side of Will. A few other knights gathered around the table, the ones carefully selected for extra protection. None of these were of the Great Knights, though most must aspire to be. Thus far, only four Great Knights existed, one for each portion of Etheland. We were planning, or at least trying to plan, what to do.

King Richard stated, "I understand you're longing to attack Akelin, Hugh, but William is right. We do not know where he or his troops are, or what his next target is."

"Do we not know this, Sire?" Edrick questioned, "Will's province was attacked, yet no one was harmed, correct?"

Levi nodded silently.

"This isn't like Akelin, is it?" Edrick went on to say. "The Akelin I've heard of is a bloodthirsty tyrant, willing to spill innocent blood even if not necessary."

"Seeing as no one was extremely harmed…" Will added, his sentence incomplete.

"Then there has to be a reason," Edrick finished. "But what?"

"Because he got weak in the knees," Hugh put gruffly.

"Close, but no," Edrick said bluntly.

"A spectacle," I responded. "He wants to get our attention."

"He's playing with us," King Richard spoke.

Edrick snapped his fingers. "Exactly."

"This still doesn't explain what he wants and where he is," Sir Hugh cried. "Have you managed to figure that out yet, you loon?"

"Uh, no, I haven't gotten that far yet," Edrick admitted.

"What if it's not just a spectacle?" Will started, bringing his hand on the map where his territory lay. "What if it's a distraction? Chaos without reason doesn't make any other sense. What if Akelin is trying to drag our attention to this, so as to keep our eyes away from the real reasoning behind his return?"

"And that is?" Edrick questioned, his expression almost mocking.

"Domination," I spoke up, putting the pieces together. "He's going to try to take back Etheland, start a rebellion." I turned to face the King, my brow creased, "He wants revenge… on you."

King Richard nodded. "I expected such. He'll be coming for me, attempting to cripple my kingdom in the process."

"Not just the kingdom," Sir Hugh announced, "but you're closest reinforcements. William is the closest to you in territory. If the castle were attacked, he'd be the one to arrive faster than any of us. Edrick is on the other side of the forest on Etheland's boundaries, and I'm all the way to the mountains. If the castle were attacked, our troops wouldn't arrive for days, even weeks."

"Even if that is the first sane thing you've said today," Edrick said, winning a fierce scowl and grumbling from Hugh, "it doesn't explain anything. If Akelin meant to cripple any reinforcements, why not slaughter the whole of Will's territory?"

"Akelin may be the enemy, but he is not stupid," the King stated. "This had to be a spectacle, a distraction. If Akelin had committed a massacre, it would lead to calling in reinforcements. Troops would be coming in from all of your territories, for Akelin would have officially declared war for

107

such a massive killing. He wanted to cause ruckus and suspicion, not full war preparation."

"What if we got this all wrong," I suggested. "Think about it. Akelin attacked a day *after* Will arrived at the castle. He waited for the Master of the house to be out of the picture before he struck. What if he used the opportunity to strike a lord-lacking territory so as to lure all the other lords together, leaving more territories without their leaders? King Richard is right in the sense that if there were a massacre, it would cause troops to be sent in, but only a meeting if it caused chaos. Akelin must know this, so he made an opportunity to summon the Great Knights away from home so as he could strike while they are away."

Sir Hugh's eyes widened, "If this is true, then that means…"

"He could be attacking right now," Edrick finished, passing a hand over his face.

Hugh fell into his seat, his face appalled. "My wife… my boy… they're at the fortress. If Akelin lays a finger on my family, I'll—!"

"We still don't know where Akelin is," Will spoke up. "We have to find him, before he takes more permanent action."

"What do you suggest, Will?" Edrick questioned, his face unreadable. "Scour the kingdom? Knock on every door until we find the adversary? Or do we just let him find us first, then?"

I didn't like the way Edrick spoke to Will as if he were the cause for these problems. Will didn't retaliate with anything but a hard glare that I was sure even I would tremble under.

Turning to the King, Will continued, "Why don't we send scouts throughout Etheland? Send some to the mountains, some to the towns and villages, and others to the forests. This way we can find where he is, where he's not, and how big his troops are *before* we attack. I also suggest increasing security around all the lords' territories, the villages, and the castle especially, just to be prepared."

"That does seem to be the wisest course of action at this moment," King Richard agreed. "Seeing as our information is limited, it is better that we prepare for an attack rather than be caught off guard when one comes. Does everyone agree?"

Will and I raised our hands, a series of others following suit. Sir Edrick was the one to raise his hand last, his face dark.

"Then it's settled," King Richard proclaimed, his face framed by the sun's light. "Send the scouts."

Sam and I walked our horses through the forest, getting some fresh air. Though the day was bright, we kept a wary eye out for Akelin's men. Who knew where they could be lurking?

The silence between us was practically unbearable, so in order to break it I asked, "Can you tell me something?"

Sam looked back at me as she responded, "Well, it depends what you want me to say."

"Tell me about your family, your life when you were a kid."

Sam gave me a questioning look.

"Unless you don't want to, or if it's too painful," I quickly added.

"No. No, it's fine." She looked down at her hands holding the reigns, a few stray red hairs falling over her face. She brought up her hand and pushed them behind her ear as she let out a deep breath. "Where would you like me to begin?"

"Who was your father?"

Sam smiled sadly. "His name was Denis Lionton. His eyes were bright green, and I inherited his red hair. Father used to smile all the time; I had such great comfort in his smile. He always had a positive attitude, even in the hardest of times. And he loved to laugh, especially at himself. He gave off the fantasy that everything was going to be all right. If only it were so." Sam took her ring from under her shirt, her thumb tracing the gold binding.

"He was a stable master, you know, raising horses and selling them to farmers and noble men and whoever else wanted a good steed. People came from all the way across Etheland to buy his horses, and they were never disappointed, never cheated out of their money. Father had morals. He'd never even think about causing anyone unfair play. He was a good, Christian man. I think King Richard and my father would have gotten along very well." A small smile twitched at the corners of her mouth. "He always told me a story at night. He had such a way with words, able to spin life into the air with only his voice. Some of his stories were complete folly, but others were quite wondrous. He enjoyed using actual people as the characters. He told tales where Hanna and I were the heroes, saving kingdoms from distress. He told of dragons and elves, and people who could

110

perform magic. My favorites were the stories of his adventures with Mother, filled with excitement and romance. I know that they couldn't be true, but it was still fantastic to imagine my parents in their youth, frolicking through fields with fairies, defending the innocent from evil lords, and even escaping the terrors of Akelin."

"What was your favorite of all the stories?" I asked, not wanting her to stop.

"Would you like me to tell it to you?" she questioned.

I nodded, finding myself enjoying the way her voice flowed as she spoke of her childhood.

"Alright," Sam gave a soft laugh. "There once was a king, an evil king, who ruled the land. He had a sister, Lillian, who was as gentle and sweet as her brother was cruel and horrid. She had long brown hair and pale blue eyes that sparkled from the joy dancing behind them. Lillian, though she loved her brother, did not love how he treated and ruled his people.

"One day the wicked king told his sister that she was to marry the captain of the guard who was only slightly less cruel than the king himself. Lillian, however, did not want anything to do with the man, let alone marry him. She was in love with the stable boy, Denis. When she told her brother that she did not wish to marry the man he had chosen for her, he was furious! He told her she would marry the captain whether she wanted to or not! She fled and told Denis what her brother had said; they agreed that they should run away. Secretly they wed, finding sanctuary in woods where they lived. In time, they had two daughters. Of course, they lived happily ever after."

I quickly snapped out of the rhythmic movement of Sam's voice and asked, "Who was the king?"

She laughed, "Oh, I don't know. It was just a bedtime story my father told me. It's not like it really happened."

I blinked. "Oh, right." It had seemed so real, I'd forgotten it was only a story. Strange, though, how did one come up with something like that? I supposed I never did get the minds of story tellers. "Tell me about your mother," I persuaded.

"Mother's name was Lillian and she did have brown hair and pale blue eyes. She really was very sweet and very kind. She kept my father tame, as she said often. She was delicate, but brave. She was only brave when she had to be, she also said often. Once when I was out picking berries with her, a wolf came out of nowhere! It growled and I screamed. It was on its hind legs and I felt so small and helpless. She just stepped right in front of me. The wolf snarled at her, but she just stood there and stared at the wolf with a firm expression. The wolf just... walked away." Sam looked up at me and I saw how her eyes were filled with joy and sadness.

I wanted to ask her more about her past. I wanted her to keep telling me her story, but her expression changed to confusion as she sniffed the air. "Do you smell that?"

I smelled the wind. "Smoke?"

Suddenly an ear piercing scream filled the air around us, causing my gut to writhe. Billy and Autumn reared back, whinnying in fright and pulling the reins away. I had to duck to keep from getting smashed in the head by hooves. Glancing up, I found Sam already on her horse, galloping away and calling back for me, "Akelin. He's found us!"

"God, please. Please no. Let everything be all right, God. Please," I prayed desperately under my breath.

My stomach twisted into knots with worry. We had it wrong, all wrong. Akelin wasn't making an opportunity to attack the lands of the Etheland. He was luring the Great Knights together so he could abolish us. I pushed Autumn faster. The smell of smoke hung heavily in the air, stinging my eyes.

I caught a glimpse of the Golden Rose before Autumn skid to a stop in front of the meeting place. It was ablaze! Flames flew across the thatched roof, trying to eat away at the house. Thank goodness for the outside walls being of stone, otherwise... Tongues of flame licked out from the windows as they found wood to devour. Men, both singed and burned, tried to run as fast as possible away from the slowly smoldering structure.

I slid off of Autumn and ran to a coughing Sir Hugh. His beard was a little singed and ash spotted over him, but he wasn't seriously injured. "Where is he?" I asked him, "Where is the King?"

Between coughs, he answered, "In the meeting room—don't know if he got out." Hugh was thrown into a fit of coughing.

Cold panic gripped my chest. Looking up at the fire licked building; I realized what needed to be done. The chill was replaced by white hot determination. With a few loud barks, I managed to quickly call forward five of the closest soldiers: two the burly warriors of Sir Hugh and three the esteemed soldiers of the castle. It didn't take much to convince them to brave the fire with me for the King.

I gave a whistle and Autumn came trotting over. I helped Sir Hugh onto her back. "She'll take you to the castle," I called to him over the roar of the fire.

Turning, I ran inside the Golden Rose before Sir Hugh could stop me, the five men right at my heels. It immediately reminded me of that tragic day twelve years ago. Flames sprouted over the walls like dancing figures, small but growing. The smoke stung my eyes and the heat sent blow after blow onto my face and arms. Ashes and embers fell in my hair.

"We need to hurry," one of Hugh's men warned beside me. "This place could collapse any second."

With a nod, I quickened my pace, entering the hallway. Hearing the crack of wood, I looked up toward the noise. As I jumped out of the way, a piece of the ceiling fell directly on the area I had just been standing! Boards and stone blocked the way back, tongues of flame roaring to form a barrier. The shouts of the others calling for me breached the crack of fire.

"I'm all right," I hollered. "I can't get through. You find another way around, I'll keep searching!"

"We won't leave you!" retorted a heavy voice.

A shower of sparks caused me to skitter back. "You will, else we're all dead!" I snapped.

When I heard no response, I almost thought they left. When I was about to run off, there was a different voice consenting, "We'll find another way."

A groan above my head was the last I heard before I moved quickly so not to be in the way of any more collapsing walls or falling ceilings.

"King Richard!" I called out, running frantically around the house, "Father! Father, where are you?"

My eyes moved every which way. A burst of sparks set off behind me. I needed to hurry. Shoving open the door to the meeting room, I searched for the King, but it was empty. My eyes scanned the floor instinctively, but I didn't find whatever it was my subconscious self looked for.

Returning to the smoke filled hall, I screamed yet again, "Father!"

"Come out, Akelin!" I heard the King's voice yell, "You can't hide forever!"

I rushed down the hallway, flying into the room where the voice came from. The King stood there, his sword drawn, searching. He shouted at the cloud of smoke circling the room.

"I know you're here!" he cried, his face contorted in a fearsome scowl. "Show yourself, you coward!"

I ran to him, avoiding his blade, "You need to get out of here."

His face turned to me in sudden concern. "Samantha, what are you doing? You shouldn't be here."

"Neither should you!" I grasped his arm. "We need to go."

He looked at me, a strange fire in his eyes. "He's here! I must find him!"

"We *will* find him, but not now. When we're back at the castle, we will search for him," I pleaded, "but not now. We have to get out of here!" Noticing the contemplation on his face, I added, "I'm not leaving without you!"

I reached out my hand. With only but a moment's hesitation, he seized it as he sheathed his sword and muttered, "You shouldn't have come."

I pulled him behind me for a while until a wall crashed in front of me, blocking our path. My eyes darted around the room. We were trapped. A chair caught my eye, and I ran to grab it, but the King got to it first. Taking it up, he smashed it against the unstable, diminishing wall again and again until finally the wall crumpled to ash.

Leading the way through the hole, I followed him through the house. The King was thrown into a fit of coughing, but still on he went. Nearing the exit, I noticed that the wooden beams started to crack and groan.

"Hurry!" I shouted.

Suddenly, a sword sliced through flames. The attacker missed the King, having misjudged the distance. Drawing my sword, I struck out at the man allowing just enough time for us to burst outside into daylight. The assailant followed, throwing himself at me and knocking me to the ground. Tumbling over, I used my sword to block his from my face. Wrestling to get him off, I heard the beams groan inside the house just to my side. An idea forming in my head, I kicked the man in the groin with my knee, leaving him off guard for the seconds I needed. I jumped up and grabbed him, sending the two of us rolling back inside the Golden Rose and into the flames.

My opponent dragged his sword down during our tumble, the blade running down my shoulder. I cried out in pain and alarm, trying desperately to get the man off. Using his own pain against him, I plunged my knee in his groin yet again, causing him to recoil and open a spot of vulnerability. I kicked out with my legs, shoving him to the door frame and away from me. Before Akelin's man could do anything, the beams gave a mighty groan and snapped. With only time for a cry in panic, the wall gave way and crushed him under stone.

Hastily I stood, face to the collapsed wall blocking the way out. Trapped and badly wounded, I clutched my bleeding shoulder and looked for something to bind it. The tapestry! It was burnt, but not destroyed. I yanked it from the wall and tore it to strips. With difficulty, I managed to wrap my shoulder, binding my injury. With no way for it to escape, smoke filled the room in a heavy cloud, causing me to cough heavily. I beat my fists against the wall, but to no avail. Trapped on all sides, I looked for anything to use as a weapon against the barrier, but there was nothing.

My vision blurred and my head spun from the smoke as well as the throbbing in my shoulder from the loss of blood. I continually pounded my fists against the stone, tears rolling down my hot face and blood dripping from my cut hands until I felt nothing and all went black.

"Whoa, Billy." I pulled back on the reigns, sliding him to a stop. I gaped from the horrid sight before my eyes. The Golden Rose was aflame! The fire hadn't taken its full affect yet, but it should grow before long. The whole house wasn't made of stone, after all. Quickly, I slipped off my horse and tethered him to the ground. I was going to need him later for certain.

"Go on, get out of here!" I turned to see a scorched Sir Hugh riding atop Sam's chestnut mare, his gaze venturing around the bustle of knights trying to either escape or search for something to put out the fire. "No use feeding water to the flames," Hugh cried. "Get on and go!"

"Hugh." I ran to him. Maybe he knew something.

"Not now, lad, I've gotta to get these blokes to the castle," he grunted.

"What happened? Where's Sam?"

"Akelin's men let loose flaming arrows on the Rose," Hugh explained. "Spread like a disease. They took back the flag, too—*you*, out!" He jabbed his finger at a knight attempting to drown the flames. After assuring the knight was on his way, Hugh turned back to me. "Sam went in for the King with some others, told me to get to the castle. Huh, like that's gonna happen!"

"Sam's in there!" I exclaimed, turning instantly for the burning house.

"Whoa there, son!" Hugh reached out and grasped my shoulder. "You need to help me get these dimwits out of here! If those two aren't back soon, we'll go in after 'em."

Shaking myself from his grip, I reluctantly relented, "Fine, but no more than two minutes before I go in."

Nodding, Hugh turned the mare away toward a group of soldiers trying to throw water on the house. "You knuckle-headed blokes! What do you think that is, a campfire?"

It didn't take long at all to get everyone heading for the castle. Most were trying to find Akelin's men or save the Golden Rose, but with one glare from Hugh or a few barks

118

of my own, they soon hightailed on out of here. From the corner of my eye, I spotted a flash of black rushing from the side of the burning house. I ran after the figure, thinking it another soldier. He bounded on foot into the forest, trailing a large, dark cloth behind him like a cape. The fabric unfurled for but a moment, revealing a silver skull, jaw trust back in a silent scream: Akelin's emblem.

"William!"

I faltered in my pursuit, glancing back at Sir Hugh on the other end of the clearing. He was running for the Golden Rose with five ash covered men, horse abandoned. Turning back to Akelin's man, I only got a last look at his foreboding cape before the enemy disappeared into the forest. Cursing under my breath, I ran after Sir Hugh.

A cry stung my ears, the clash of metal against metal. A horrible crash echoed through the glade, mingling with the snapping of flames. Before I even saw them, I could only imagine who was fighting. As soon as I reached the front of the house, I took in the sight. Hugh just felled his attacker and another lay dead on the ground, the King's sword in his abdomen. The King doubled over, coughing heavily as he stumbled to the blocked door. Without thinking, I grabbed hold of him, keeping him back from the flames. The King struggled against my grip as I did mine, neither of us gaining any ground.

"I must go back. I must go back in there," King Richard persisted, his tone dangerous.

"No, Sire! Your safety is our first priority," I explained. "You can't go back in there!"

"You don't understand, boy." He threw into another fit of coughing, making him double over yet again, falling against my hold. "My daughter… my daughter is still in there!"

A sense of urgency squeezed my chest. I had to get King Richard to safety, but Sam… I must save her. Spotting a horse wandering around, I ran to it and snatched its reigns and led it back to the King despite the panic in the beast's eyes.

"Go to the castle. I'll get Sam and we will meet you there," I told him.

"No," he stated bluntly. "That is *my daughter* in there. I'm going in with you."

"You can't!" I protested. "With all due respect, I can't allow you to risk your life like this."

The fire in King Richard's eyes sent a chill down my spine. "Over my dead body."

Groaning in exasperation, I knew that nothing I said would get the King on the horse. Reluctantly, I grunted in consent.

Sir Hugh slapped me on the back. "Nice try, lad. Pointless, but nice try."

Whirling around, I looked for a way to get inside the house, the King right behind me. The entrance was blocked by stone that fell over it, prohibiting anyone from getting in or out.

"Is there any other way to get in?" I questioned the King.

"Back door, on the left," he answered, never breaking stride as we traveled around the house.

King Richard reached it first, followed by Hugh and me. The fire almost completely covered the entrance, hiding the inside from view. Just as the King ducked his head to charge through the flames, I heard the crack and scatter of wood.

Grabbing the King by the collar, I pulled him back full force just as the ceiling collapsed over the doorway.

"Thank you, son," the King heaved out as he struggled to his feet.

"How do we get in now?" Hugh questioned.

My eyes scanned the wall, searching for any way to enter. Flames continually devoured at the plaster between the stone, keeping any entrance hidden. My gaze fell on a small opening, a window of some sort at the second floor of the house. It must have been left open before the fire, or maybe that was the way the intruders got in. Either way, it was the only means of getting inside.

"There." I pointed it out to the others. "If we can just get up there, we could get in."

King Richard nodded. "Alright, we'll give you a boost. You get Sam while Hugh and I get this door exposed for you two to get out. Now, hurry."

With hands folded and ready to give me just the extra height I needed, the King and Sir Hugh stayed as a base for just enough time for me to grab onto the window sill. Pulling myself up, I fell through the opening, immediately surrounded by smoke. The heat pounded against my face and arms as the smoke burned my eyes. Cinders and ashes already started to attach themselves to me.

I started running, my feet pounding against the floor. "Sam!" I continually cried. "Sam!"

My foot fell through the diminishing floor. I dropped, landing in a heap on the first floor among the smoldering wood and dusty remnants. Shaking off the ashes on my face, I struggled to regain my footing. A sharp pain shot up my right ankle, crippling me for a few seconds. Limping as fast as I could, I continued down the fire ridden hall, shouting for Sam. My smarting eyes looked every which way.

"Sam!" I cried again, and I heard a whimper. Could it have been my imagination? I couldn't take any chances. I stomped my injured foot against the door before me, driving my heel right beside the damaged lock. Despite the pain, I repeated the kick until the door broke off its hinges and crashed to the ground. "Sam!"

My gaze scanned the room until I spotted her lying almost unconscious on the floor. Ash and embers covered her like a blanket. A strip of tapestry was wrapped around her shoulder, blood seeping through it from a wound. Her hands were cut and bleeding, probably from pounding them against the wall.

I ran to her. "Sam, I'm going to get you out of here. We're going to get out, just stay with me," I whispered as I gingerly picked up her limp body. She was much lighter than I expected.

A piece of the ceiling fell just a few feet away. I stood up with Sam cradled in my arms and started back the way I came. I ran as fast as my twisted ankle allowed, whispering a prayer to God to get us out of here and not take Sam home, not yet. Sparks sprayed everywhere; the flames had grown dangerously, now. I turned one way, but quickly turned the other as a wardrobe blocked the first.

Finally, I saw the hole in the wall that had once been the back door. I darted for it despite the hurt, holding Sam close. King Richard's form came into view just beyond the opening, still working at exposing the doorway with Sir Hugh. I leapt through the hole and into warm sunshine as I heard another wall crash behind me.

Chapter Thirteen

I opened my eyes a little and found myself looking up into Will's face. My chest heaved, lungs burning as I coughed heavily. I felt the bouncing gallop of a horse as it carried us away to who knew where. My head pounded, my vision blurred. Thick ashen gunk flavored the back of my tongue. Will mumbled something, his expression worried. Before I could figure out why, darkness engulfed me once again.

"Almost there. We're almost there," I whispered under my breath.

My legs were the only things keeping me up right on top of Billy and the only things steering as well. My arms were busy trying to support Sam and apply pressure to her wound, just like she did for my hawk puncture wounds. King Richard and Sir Hugh rode ahead of me, leading the way out of the forest and away from the Golden Rose.

"How is she?" the King called back to me.

"Holding on," I responded, keeping my tone calm and even.

King Richard only looked forward, hiding his face from sight. I knew he was worried. I was too. I brushed Sam's hair away from her sooty face, my hand returning to her shoulder in an instant to stop the bleeding. The blood still seeped through my fingers and stained my hand red. I leaned forward to better secure my hold on her and to stay atop my horse.

The castle finally came into view. I urged Billy to go faster, digging my heels into his sides even as one ankle started to swell. Men swarmed outside the castle; most appeared to be receiving aid. Levi seemed to be refusing treatment as he watched for us. The Queen was there, watching with the old knight for our coming. When she spotted us, her face relaxed in relief. As we drew nearer, however, her face shifted.

King Richard leaped off his horse before he came to a full stop. "Where is the physician?" He exclaimed, "I need to see him now!"

An elderly man stepped out of the bustle of people. "Yes?"

I bid Billy to stop as I slid off his back with Sam hanging limp in my arms. "It's Sam. She's hurt!"

The King took his daughter from my arms, practically flying into the castle with the physician following him in suit. All I could do was stare after them, no longer aware of the throbbing in my ankle. A servant girl took me by the hand and beckoned me to sit. I obeyed subconsciously.

The Queen ran to my side, asking me a steam of questions that I replied without real knowledge of my saying anything. My mind was a haze. All I could think about was Sam and the way her face looked pallid when they took her away—just as my mother's had, just as my father's had, so many years ago. Dead.

The only awareness I was capable of was a raging, burning heat. It hazed my vision when I opened my eyes and seared behind my lids when I closed them. Fire seemed to flower under my skin, causing my heart to throb rather than beat. It was in this flaming blaze that visions of inferno flicked through my mind. Orange fingers of flame stroked crimson sprays of blood. Screams from unknown lips rang in my ears as if a battle waged all around me, but only the flash of a blade or the shine of armor was visible through the fire.

And just as quickly as the furnace began, so did it end. Cold shot down my limbs, ice freezing my blood. Flakes fell around me like snow, but it wasn't snow. It was ash. The gray flecks covered the floor like a blanket. An invisible wind brushed them past still faces and forms pale as powder. Frosty shivers traveled down my body, both from the chill and from the grief... and the fear. Muscles stiffening, my teeth chattered. A lone figure, a simple silhouette through the swirl of ashes, stood across from me in the bitter gloom.

Before my eyes could focus, a blast of heat hit my face and the fire returned with a vengeance.

"I just don't understand how this could have happened?" Sir Edrick emphasized, "Only a hand full of knights, and the royal family of course, knew about the Golden Rose and its location! How could *he* know about it?"

"More importantly," Levi indicated, "how did Akelin know we were meeting there in that short of a time?"

"There must be a traitor in our midst!" Sir Hugh declared.

"How is that so, Hugh? I am sure no one here would do such a thing," Edrick responded. "I am most certain of it."

"What would make you believe that assumption?" Hugh burst.

"Well, I know for a fact His Majesty, the King, did not inform Akelin of the whereabouts of the Golden Rose. And I am most positive the Princess, as well as the Queen, did not do this dreadful deed. Sir Levi has served his time as a knight of King Richard, and he wouldn't betray his country to the enemy of the King. And though I have just met Will, I am sure he would not do this. The knights who attended for witness and for protection did not know enough about the matter at hand to tell about it. I most defiantly did not become a traitor to King Richard. Unless *you*, Sir Hugh, did this…"

"I most certainly did not!" Hugh shouted.

"Then I rest my case." Edrick took a seat with a content expression on his face.

Hugh scowled at Edrick. I only stared into empty space, listening to the voices around the room. My mind seemed to have slowed to a complete stop. I knew I had to be here, but more than anything I just wanted to check on Sam. No news had come to me in the past few hours since we arrived. The King should be here any minute, hopefully with some indication of Sam's state. Until then, I might go mad.

"All this gathering seems to be telling us is what we don't know," Sir Hugh grumbled.

"That's not entirely true," Sir Levi spoke. "This goes to show what Akelin's plans were for attacking the territory of Sir William."

"And what is that, Sir Levi?" Edrick questioned, his tone testy.

"Well, it was just as the Princess had said," Levi explained. "We only misinterpreted her meaning. Instead of luring the most powerful people in Etheland together so as to attack their territories, he wanted to lure us together to attack us all at once."

"I suppose that does make sense," Edrick admitted.

"And did you see the flag?" Sir Levi asked, his voice just above a whisper.

"Aye," Sir Hugh nodded gravely, his eyes filled with terror. "I saw it. The intruders raised it above the flames, giving off that bloody cry of Akelin. Twas the most terrible thing these eyes have ever seen."

"The fire made the skull look all the more horrifying," Levi added, his eyes also haunted, "the fabric never even smoldered as they carried it through the flames."

"Awe, rubbish," Edrick mocked. "You two talk like the banner is accursed. From your stories, folks would think the thing's alive."

A shadow passed over Levi's face, foreboding eyes fixed on Edrick. He pointed a scolding finger at the knight. "Do not underestimate the power in that emblem, boy. I worked in the mines of Akelin where they branded their workers." Levi yanked up his sleeve, exposing his forearm. On his skin were striking white scars in the shape of Akelin's emblem. "I see the Screaming Skull every day. You don't know what that sign does to a man, what *Fear* does to a man. When the most evil of fears comes back from the grave, it makes a man very desperate, very *dangerous*."

Edrick's face revealed slight intimidation. Levi's words made me tremble, even in my silent emptiness. I remembered the stories the old knight used to tell me about his past. He worked in the mines since he was a boy, forced to because his father had rebelled against Akelin. He was branded with the emblem as a child like a slave. Levi worked until he was a young man, escaping to join the rebellion led by King Richard. He fought against the man who had taken his freedom and spent the rest of his youth fighting for the man who gave it back.

"Akelin is not a man, Sir Edrick," Levi continued, returning to his place and pulling his sleeve over the wretched brand. "He is a demon."

The doors opened wide and we all stood. King Richard entered, his expression exhausted. His beard was singed and his face was burned, though not too badly. His hands were bandaged from the scratches and blisters he'd gotten in tearing away the barrier so Sam and I could get out of the building. The clothes he wore were the same as before, blackened with soot and scorched at the edges. He had not changed much since I saw him last.

"Your Highness," I requested. "May I speak?"

"Yes, quickly though," the King relented, his voice gruff. "I have much to state."

"How," I began, pausing briefly for the catch in my throat, "how is your daughter?"

His expression softened. "She is still not conscious. The doctor is seeing to her."

I sighed, relief flooding through me. Sam's alive. She's going to be all right.

King Richard turned to the whole of us, his proclamation full of passion and almost anger, "Akelin has been in hiding for too long! We must end this! We will continue with the original plan, strengthening security throughout the entire kingdom. The scouts must move quickly. Edrick, send yours to all of the forests. You will inform them to look behind every tree for any sign of the traitor. Hugh, send yours to the mountains. They are to leave no stone unturned and are not to return empty handed until absolutely certain of him not being there. William, your scouts will join with mine in the search through the towns and villages. You and Sam will lead them together. We will check everywhere!"

"And me, Your Majesty?" Sir Levi questioned, his stature the bravest and most cunning I'd ever seen. He didn't seem like the old man I had known all my life, the retired knight with a bad leg. He now looked like a warrior, ready for battle as if he never left the army.

"I will need you, my old friend." King Richard placed a hand on Levi's shoulder. "I need the people I trust most. You will stay with me, organizing preparations for battle. If you, of course, are willing to join the ranks of the Great Knights once again."

"Long ago I swore to serve my King and my country until I breathe my last," Sir Levi stated. "I intend on keeping it."

King Richard smiled, facing us once again. "My Great Knights, if it is war Akelin seeks then it is war he shall find!"

"Let's send this demon back to the fiery gates of his master!" Hugh bellowed.

Chapter Fourteen

I woke up in a cold sweat and found myself looking into a pair of green eyes. My first thought was that it was my father looking down on me with such concern and love. As my mind focused on the now, I knew that it wasn't him. Father was dead. These eyes did not belong to him, but to Will. My heart pounded rapidly, my breathing heavy and quick. Will took a rag and dipped it into a bowl of icy water. He took the now wet rag and lightly dabbed my hot forehead with it. I cringed, a searing pain stabbing at the touch.

"It's all right. It was just a dream," he soothed.

"A nightmare is more like it," I responded; my voice sounded weak and broken to my own ears. "Why does it hurt?"

"You have some pretty bad burns, Sam," Will answered though I could tell that he toned it down for my sake. From the pain all over, I obviously had more than a few.

Looking around, I recognized my room. I never thought my bed could be so comfortable and yet so uncomfortable. Every time I moved, a sharp pain in my shoulder surfaced. I reached up, touching the bandages. If I was right, it was stitched up. My gaze continued to roam when they fell on the small flames burning in the fireplace.

My chest convulsed as I was thrown into the events that occurred at the Golden Rose, my body jolting in turn from the impact. I groaned from the pain in my shoulder and the ache of my seized muscles as I was thrust back into the present just as abruptly. Agony took hold again. I felt every burn on my being, the flames seeming to still be licking my skin.

Will hushed me, trying to calm me down. I forced my breaths to steady. Closing my eyes, I attempted to relax my muscles and brush the spasm away, ashamed of allowing the anxiety to get the better of me.

"How long have I been unconscious?" I asked, opening my eyes.

"You've been in and out of consciousness for almost two weeks," he responded, putting the rag and bowl of water aside. "You had quite a fever, Sam. The physician was relieved when it finally broke, and he was afraid it might return."

Two weeks? But it's only been a few hours since the Golden Rose. What's gone on since then? "What happened?" I questioned.

"The King is safe if that's what you mean. He, Hugh and I got you out of the Golden Rose and brought you back here. One of the servant girls stitched up that gash in your shoulder, which you got *how*, exactly?"

I managed to force a smile. "One of Akelin's followers came and attacked. We had a bit of a scramble and his sword scraped my shoulder."

"Scraped?" Will raised an eyebrow.

"I'm all right, aren't I?" I shrugged. "Anyway, I shoved him away just as a wall fell on top of him. You know the rest."

"I see," Will sighed.

"Speaking of King Richard," I acknowledged, "where is he?"

"He was here a couple of hours ago. He would have stayed much longer, but the Queen *insisted* he needed to rest." He smiled. "So I'm here instead."

"Ah, yes. The Queen can be a bit... *stubborn* sometimes." I grinned. Will looked down at my hands and I noticed the bandages for the first time. "I was pounding the wall, trying to get out, but *apparently* the only things that got affected were my own fists," I explained.

Will opened his mouth to respond, but a scratching on the door interrupted him. He looked quizzical. The scuffing stopped, replaced by a series of whimpers. The scratching started up again, accompanied by a pitiful yowl.

I giggled. "Won't you let the poor thing in? Who *knows* what scared ideas are running through her mind?"

Will smiled as he got up and opened the door. A streak of tan and black fur bolted through the door and ran to my side. A pink tongue was suddenly licking my face!

"Down, girl. Megs get down!" I said in between laughing, "I know, I know. I missed you, too. I'm all right, girl."

Megs stopped licking my face, putting her front paws on the bed and resting her head on top of them. Her tail wagged so fast, it was just a blur. I reached over to scratch between her ears. She sniffed my bandaged hand and gave a little whimper.

I looked up at Will, who returned to his chair next to my bed. "Two weeks you said I was out? That should be enough time for my hands to heal, at least enough time not to need bandages," I acknowledged. I tried to unwrap one bandaged hand, but it was trickier than I thought since my other was bandaged as well.

"Here, let me," Will offered.

I allowed him to take my hand with only brief hesitation. As he gently removed the bandages and soon both of my hands were unwrapped, I looked at them and noted the scabs and the red irritation where my skin was burned. Thank goodness they used my burn cream. Otherwise, my hands would be in a much worse state than they were now. They weren't healed, not all the way at least, but it wasn't so bad that I needed the bandages any more. It was definitely not as bad as I'd thought.

I reached over and scratched under my German Shepherd's chin. She tickled my fingers with her tongue.

"Thank you," I said softly.

"No problem," Will replied.

"I wasn't talking about my hands," I whispered. "I meant about saving me."

"I know," he responded softly.

I raised my eyes up to his and gave a little smile. Will smiled back.

"Well," he stood up, "now that you are awake, I will go and inform the King of your condition. Besides, I can see you're well taken care of." He gestured to Megs.

"Alright," I said. Megs' eyes followed Will until he was out of the room. As soon as the door shut behind him, Megs jumped up on the bed beside me and rested her head on my torso.

Taking sanctuary in my designated bedchamber, I stared out the window at the sleeping city below. Stars blinked down from the sky framing a pale crescent moon, all still visible despite the gray blush spreading over the horizon. A lone cart rolled down the street, probably to sell goods at market. With a sigh, I rubbed my sleepless eyes and turned from the sight. Movement caught my gaze in the dim room.

"Who's there?" I inquired.

The strike of flint and the flashing light of a candle revealed a dark haired, freckled boy, his brown eyes shining in the light.

"John?" I questioned.

He was near unrecognizable, his face so solemn with worry. Dark circles hung under his eyes indicating that he too had little sleep of late.

"What's wrong?"

Wringing his hands, John seemed to find trouble getting his words out. "A man of the survivors, one who came from your territory seeking homage here," he started, his words carefully chosen. "He sent me a message from a friend back home; that is, my family's home in Sir Edrick's territory."

I recalled John's origins, how he was sent to my house to serve as my page and squire. I'd nearly forgotten that my friend had family still across the forest.

"In the message, she said that things are happening back home, strange things," John continued. "She did not specify exactly what, but she asked that I... return there to help."

My heart dropped, but I said nothing.

Lifting his gaze, he stated, "I know that my duty and loyalties are here with you as my master and friend, especially in this threatening time..." His shoulders straightened. "But I also have a duty and loyalty to my family and people. Sir, they need me. I do not know why, but I believe them to be in trouble. My friend would not request my presence otherwise."

Still I said nothing, my mind racing at the prospects of John's proposal.

"I have thought about this for a time now," John confessed. "I didn't think it wise to leave while you were away, or while you needed me with the survivors. But I'm afraid that if I wait too long it'll be too late. However... I understand if you deem it best that I stay here. I know that of all the times I've been in your apprenticeship, this is the time you may need me most. In which case, I understand if you deny my request to return to my home until matters are taken care of. I only ask that someone be sent to attend to my friend's pleading call."

I sighed, understanding the gravity of this request and the stature in which John came about it. He wished to go, that much was certain. Whether he should go, I supposed that was for me to decide. I didn't want him to leave, but I knew that I had no real excuse for John not to return to his home. This was too important to him. Would I not do the same if I were in his shoes? No, I realized, I would have left without even asking permission.

With a sigh, I concluded, "This is important to you, yes?"

John nodded. "Yes, very much so."

"And your friend, you trust him in that he would only ask for you if it were important?"

A twinge of a smile flicked at his mouth. "Yes, she would."

Raising my eyebrows, I suppressed a smile. "In that case, it seems to me that you are in greater need elsewhere than you are here with me. However, I will request that one of either the King's or Sir Hugh's men accompany you on your journey. I will personally speak to one of them, and have the servants pack your saddlebags and ready your steed. You may go when the sun reaches its peak, but until then," I took a seat beside the candle's glow, "tell me of this *friend* of yours."

John laughed, sitting before me, the joy and gratitude evident in his eyes. "We grew up together," he began. "She's adopted, though it's easy to forget with how close she was with her adopted parents. She loved venturing the forest, had a bit of a free spirit I suppose. She's gentle, everyone says, but I've seen her when she's otherwise. Strong willed, sharp tongued, especially with the other boys in the village who either pick on her or someone else. She wants to be a healer, you know. The girl who grew up climbing trees and fighting with wooden swords wants to help mend bones and stitch wounds." John's gaze drifted to the candle, his voice far away. "She loves to dance frivolously with bare feet and ribbons in her dark hair. Her laugh is full and true, but she isn't afraid to hide her tears. And her eyes are as blue as the autumn sky after the rains have beaten the earth."

His voice slipped to silence and eyes saw a face I knew not. As the light of dawn leaked into the room, I grinned. "You speak as if you're in love, my friend."

With a small laugh, John admitted, "Perhaps I am."

"You *have* to come! It wouldn't be the same without you," Nancy pleaded as we walked down the castle hall from breakfast.

"I really do want to come, honestly I do. It's just that I need to help with the search for Akelin. Trust me, I would do *anything* to be your maid of honor, but I just don't know if I'll be able to," I tried to explain.

"But what if the King would let you have just one day off for the wedding? Now that Garrick is better and the house is complete, we are more than ready to be married. We were talking, and we decided to move up the wedding so as you could attend. You have done so much for us, it would mean the world if you would come." Nancy's eyes filled with pleading and emotion. "Please, Sam? Won't you come?"

I sighed, "I'll see what I can do, but no promises."

A huge grin appeared on her face. "Oh yes! I just know the King will let you! He is such a good king, he will understand. Maybe you could bring that charming young knight of yours as well." Nancy winked at me.

I laughed, "First of all, Will is not *mine*. Second of all…" but before I finished, Nancy skipped off to do more preparations for her wedding tomorrow.

I shook my head, smiling as I started on my way to the throne room to find the King. Once I arrived, I stood before him, but he didn't notice me. He bent over some papers, studying them intently. I coughed a little. He looked up and dropped the paper in his hand. I hadn't seen him for two weeks, not since the night of the fire. He'd seen me, of course, while I was unconscious. He looked pale and tired.

"Father, if you are not too busy…" my voice trailed off as I suddenly found myself in the King's warm embrace.

He kissed the top of my head. "I'm so glad you're all right," King Richard whispered. "I was so scared. I thought I had lost you."

"You will *never* lose me," I said as I returned his embrace. A few tears fell on my head. As he pulled away, I saw them glistening on his cheeks. He smiled at me and I returned the smile.

"Now, what was it you wanted to ask me?" King Richard asked as he sat back in his throne.

"Oh, yes. Well, you see, Nancy and Garrick are getting married tomorrow and Nancy—I mean—*I* was wondering if I could have the day off. Just until the wedding is over! Then I'll be back to attend to my duties," I said quickly.

"Of course you can attend the wedding! Levi and I will see to the scouts tomorrow. You should go, enjoy yourself. Why don't you go tell Will to take the day off too? I am sure he will be thankful for a break." His eyes twinkled.

"Thank you, Father! I'll go tell him now." Giddy, I left the room.

Now to find Will. I was pretty sure I knew where he was, though. First, I found the scribe and told him to inform Nancy that I would be attending.

Walking down the hall, I stopped right before the passage turned. Sighing, I cautiously walked around the corner, but my caution did not help me, for I found myself bumping into—quite literally—my friend as usual.

Walking too fast, I ran into Sam, nearly knocking her over. I instinctively grasped her around the waist to keep her from staggering, all too aware of how close we were.

"Sorry," I apologized, stepping back as my face grew hot.

"I knew I would bump into you here." Sam smiled. "I was just hoping that this time it wouldn't be so literal."

I laughed, "So you *knew* you would find me here. Why did you want to find me?"

"I was just with the King, and he told me to tell you that we can have the day off tomorrow. He said that you would be grateful for a break."

"Well, I wouldn't want to disappoint him." I smiled. It had been a little chaotic lately. The scouts hadn't found anything yet and I'd been so busy trying to prepare my men for battle that I hadn't had much time to catch my breath.

"I wanted to ask if you would like to attend a wedding tomorrow? Nancy told me to ask you if you would." Sam bit her lip.

"Who's getting married, may I ask?"

"Garrick Hunter and Nancy Hart," she informed. "Garrick was the patient King Richard was talking about when we went hawking."

"You never *did* tell me what happened," I acknowledged.

"He got glass in his leg when he was putting in a window in the cottage he was building. He's all better now," Sam explained. "Will you come?"

"Hmm…" I rubbed my chin thoughtfully.

"Oh, come on! It will be fun!" Sam pleaded. "Besides, Elizabeth and the kids will be there, being Nancy's cousin and all."

"Why didn't you say so in the first place?" I grinned. "Count me in."

Her face glowed. "Excellent! I need to go. Millie needs to know about the wedding."

With that, she disappeared down the hall. Laughing, I continued on my way to find John so as to tell him of Hugh's agreement to have one of his most trusted men accompany my friend to his home town. I then realized something. I thought that was the longest time I had ever seen Sam smile.

Chapter Fifteen

"You look *gorgeous*, Cousin Nancy!" Isabel exclaimed.

"Oh, doesn't she?" Millie agreed.

"That Garrick is a lucky man." Bertha smiled.

"I have to agree with you, Bertha," I said.

Nancy blushed. "Oh, you are all just saying that."

"No we are *not*!" Elizabeth corrected, squeezing her cousin's shoulder, "Every bit of it is true. You are stunning! And you better believe it!"

"Thank you, Elizabeth," Nancy said softly.

It was the day of the wedding and the girls and I were getting ready. Nancy did look very pretty. Her blue eyes sparkled with a joy beyond compare and she couldn't seem to stop smiling. Her brown hair was pinned up, allowing ringlets to slip out and frame her face. Tiny silk butterflies scattered about the top of her head. Her dress was white with little flowers embroidered on the side of the torso and stretched up around her neck line. The sleeves ended just past her elbow and the skirt flowed around her when she walked. All in all, Nancy was breathtakingly beautiful!

"I am *so* glad you were able to come," Nancy said to me.

"So am I," I responded.

A knock on the door grabbed our attention. "Come in," Nancy called.

The door opened, and much to our surprise, King Richard stepped in. "Why, Your Highness!" Nancy curtsied, stunned.

The King held up a hand as if to brush aside the formalities. His eyes moved my way and I caught a wink as he smiled. Something was up his sleeve, I could tell.

"With all due respect, Sire," Nancy asked humbly, "why are you here?"

"I have heard that your father was unable to make it to the wedding, due to certain circumstances," he began sympathetically. Nancy nodded, lowering her eyes. The King continued, "Hence, I would like to ask if I may have the incredible honor of escorting the bride down the aisle. Call it a wedding present, it you must."

Nancy's eyes filled with tears but a smile was on her face. "Oh, it would be *my* honor, Sire!"

The King extended his hand and Nancy took it as if she was in a dream. As I handed Nancy the bouquet of flowers, I smiled in thanks at the King for making this day even more special for her. Her father had died a few months back. It had been such a heartbreaking moment for her; I knew, for I was there when she received the news. I couldn't believe King Richard was willing to walk Nancy down the aisle when she otherwise would have to go down it alone. I wondered how much he went through so he would be able to perform this kindness. I smiled to myself at this thought: I wasn't the only one who went beyond their limits sometimes.

"What are we waiting for?" Millie proclaimed, "It's time for the bride to meet her groom!"

The emptiness of John's departure was still fresh on my mind, despite it being a day since he left for Edrick's territory. At least he wasn't alone on his journey, seeing as Sir Hugh permitted one of his men to accompany John. I hoped he would be all right and all was well with his family and friend. With a slight smile, I realized I never asked the name of the girl John seemed to have feelings for. I would have to ask him when he returned.

Sitting in the pews of the church, I continued to wait for the bride to arrive. The groom was already standing in front of the altar with a bright smile on his face and happiness in his eyes. Elizabeth entered the room with baby Samantha in her arms and sat down in one of the pews.

Soon after, the music began to play a melodious song. I rose with the rest of the guests to watch as little Isabel walked down the aisle, scattering rose petals across the floor. Owen followed her, a pillow in his hands with two rings atop it. As he passed me, his face brightened and he wiggled his fingers to indicate a little wave. I smiled in turn.

The bride's maids and groom's men followed right after. Sam's friend, I believed her name was Millie, was one of the bride's maids who came in. She took her spot at the front of the church, waiting for the bride. The best man followed by the maid of honor, Sam, walked down the aisle. She wore a rose colored cotton dress with a faint cream trim. Her long, red hair lay in waves down her back. Sam looked, to be honest, very beautiful. She walked down the aisle and came to a stop next to Millie.

The music changed, the tone deepened, and all eyes turned to the bride. The guests gave off a small gasp. The King himself was escorting Nancy down the aisle! Though the gasp was definitely given partly because of this fact, it was also given for how stunning Nancy looked. As far as brides went, she was definitely a beautiful one.

Nancy stopped at the head of the aisle before the altar. Garrick lifted the veil from her face and she smiled at him with such love and admiration that all could see that there was no doubt in the world that they loved each other.

The priest cleared his throat before he began, "Dearly beloved, we are gathered here today to celebrate the union of this man and this woman under God..." As the declaration went on, I didn't hear most of the words, though I knew them fairly well. I attended a few weddings before, most for relatives I barely knew. Before long, the vows began.

"I, Garrick Hunter, take you, Nancy Hart, to be my wife," Garrick said, the words coming from his mouth easily yet nervously. "I promise to be true to you in good times and in bad, in sickness and in health. I will love you and honor you all the days of my life." He put the ring on his bride's finger.

Tears of joy already brimmed Nancy's eyes. "I, Nancy Hart, take you, Garrick Hunter, to be my husband." She slipped a golden band on the fourth finger of Garrick's left hand. "I promise to be true to you in good times and in bad, in sickness and in health. I will love you and honor you all the days of my life."

The priest smiled and declared, "By the power vested in me under God, I now pronounce you, husband and wife. You may now kiss the bride."

Garrick grabbed Nancy by the waist and brought her close. Nancy giggled before their lips pressed together to form a symbol of their undying, unbreakable bond of love. Everyone cheered.

"Congratulations, again!" I praised.

"Oh, thank you," Nancy smiled. "I am so happy that I would jump for joy if this dress didn't forbid it."

We both laughed. A sense of forlorn washing over me, I sighed, "I'm going to miss you, Nancy."

"I am going to miss you, as well."

"Well, what about me?" Garrick exclaimed good naturedly, "Won't anyone miss me?"

I laughed, "I'm going to miss you, too, Garrick!"

Now content, Garrick smiled, sneaking his arm around his newlywed's waist.

King Richard came up to us and said, "Congratulations, dear girl. May God be with you while you are away."

Nancy blushed. "Thank you, Your Highness." As the King departed, she turned to me, speaking softly, "We might not be back from Garrick's cousin in Lynnia until this battle is over. It is not easy to cross borders while a war is raging. Let's pray that it will be a quick one."

"Yes," I agreed, "we all hope so."

Garrick whispered something in Nancy's ear. She nodded. "We'd best be going." I suddenly found myself in Nancy's warm embrace. "Be careful, and don't forget me," she whispered in my ear.

"Don't you worry, I'll be all right," I whispered back. "I could *never* forget you. Don't speak such nonsense!"

Nancy smiled as she pulled away. "Good-bye."

"No, you know I don't like good-byes! Until next time," I corrected.

Nancy and Garrick turned and headed to the wagon waiting for them. Nancy stopped and exclaimed, "Oh, I almost forgot! I need to toss the bouquet!"

All the girls gathered around behind Nancy like a swarm of bees, arms stretched out to receive the bouquet that would soon fly through the air. Millie grabbed my hand and dragged me with the others. I reluctantly let her, laughing from her excitement.

"What is the point of this anyway?" I asked Millie.

"It's tradition! The bride throws the bouquet and whoever catches it is *supposedly* the next to get married," Millie explained.

"I know what the *point* of this is! What I don't get is why we're over here! I mean, it's just a silly old wives tale."

"But it's fun!" Millie countered.

"Yeah, well maybe, but…"

"Just hold out your hands!" Millie ordered.

I reluctantly extended my hands. "Alright, now what?"

Suddenly, a bouquet of flowers fell in my arms. I stared at it, wide eyed. Looking up, I saw Will behind the group of girls looking right back at me. I quickly passed the bouquet to Millie who, with a rather stunned expression, accepted the flowers, although I didn't think she knew what was going on. The crowd never seemed to notice that I was really the one who caught the flowers, everyone except Millie and Will. I turned to hide my blushed face.

Nancy and Garrick climbed into the horse-drawn wagon, the crowd waving their hands and handkerchiefs. Tears of joy and happiness shed at the farewell. Nancy looked right at me, tears in her eyes, and mouthed the words *good bye*.

I shook my head and muttered, "No, not good bye; until next time."

She nodded as if she heard me, smiling softly. I watched in a daze as the wagon rode away over the hills and out of my sight, taking Nancy away with it.

It was probably for their own good that they married when they did. It was also probably for their own good that they were leaving now, headed for a different country with no war. They'll probably be safer there for the time being. For this kind of day, filled with peace and happiness, may not occur again for a long time. This was probably their only chance to be bound by the bond of marriage, and they knew it, so they took it. The days such as this one were limited, for the war to defeat Akelin and restore peace to Etheland had only begun.

Chapter Sixteen

"How is the progress coming along?" King Richard asked.

"I've sent my scouts to the mountains once again. They'll report back to me the moment they find that rotten Akelin and his band of Screaming Skull lovers!" Sir Hugh exclaimed.

"Please, Sir Hugh. Save this energy and hatred for the battle yet to come," Sam said calmly, concealing the sorrow I sensed in her voice.

Hugh grouchily grasped his mug and took a big gulp of the bitter liquid inside, the drops dribbling down over his beard. We'd received news of two more attacks in the past week alone. A town near Sir Hugh's territory was torched, this time burning twelve innocent people to death. An attack on a village closer to the forest left seven more dead, everyone else wounded in some form or fashion. In each setting, the reports said that the flag of Akelin was carried high through the flames.

"Edrick, how is the progress coming?" King Richard turned to him.

"I will be joining my scouts in the forest soon. I will inform you, Your Majesty, when we have found Akelin," Sir Edrick stated calmly.

I looked at him questionably. I could tell he was hiding something. I knew it the moment I first saw him. He was daring, a little *too* daring. His demeanor didn't hold the same urgency and hatred as the rest of us.

Hugh was particularly antsy, his anger toward Akelin clearly visible. Levi was digging into the papers littered in front of him like a greedy dog, looking for any clues of Akelin and his uprising. King Richard's temper—though controlled and orderly—was obviously determined and firm, waiting for anything to which he could take action upon. Sam was the most composed of all of us, her emotion and urgency hidden behind those striking eyes.

As for me, Akelin's very name made me shudder, the image of Sam's pale and seemingly dead face coming to mind at the mere thought of him. But Edrick, his behavior was all too collected, especially after recently hearing of the deaths of nineteen people. The smirk at the corner of his mouth was far too constant, and for no particular reason. I couldn't help but feel like his lips dripped with honey when he spoke. When he smiled, it was like a crocodile's smile, tempting but dangerous and misleading. His gaze lay on Sam longer than necessary and more often than typical. I didn't like him and I definitely didn't trust him.

Edrick caught me eying him and didn't act like he noticed. I shoved my suspicions to the back of my mind and stopped.

"Sam and I will be checking in on the scouts soon," I informed the King.

"Good," the King said, his tone reveling his passion and determination. "Soon, we will find this devil who dares to

151

call himself a man! I will not take any more of his barbarous acts. This time, he will not escape so easily."

I walked down the hallway, Will on one side, Megs on the other. "So, how long have you known Sir Edrick?" Will asked me after a length of silence.

"Since he became a knight," I replied. "He's not much older than you and I, you know. He's twenty-six, only five years older than I and three older than you. I'm not close to him; I only see him when he comes to the castle. I don't know him enough to visit him. The King is fond of him, though. Why do you ask?"

"Oh, just curious," Will responded.

"I am more familiar with Sir Hugh, however," I smiled amusingly. "He has wanted more than once a rematch for whatever! He's very competitive and does not enjoy defeat. He was the one who trained me to be a knight. He's like an uncle to me, in some ways. He may seem tough on the outside, but he really is very nice and funny. He can be easy to get along with once you get to know him." I paused, rethinking, "You just don't want to be on his bad side."

"And who is on his bad side, might I ask?"

"Well, he is not fond of Edrick. He tends to get on Hugh's nerves a lot."

"Edrick does have that affect on people," Will muttered, glancing up. "Speaking of…"

I turned my head to see Edrick coming up the hall towards us.

"Hello, Princess. I am glad to see you well again." He smiled at me, making me feel a bit uneasy. He turned to Will and briefly said, "Hello, Will." I couldn't help but hear a bit of dryness in his voice.

Megs tensed under my hand on her back. The hairs on her neck stood on end, ears lying flat on her head. Her lips curling up into a snarl, she gave a dreadful growl.

"Megs?" I said quizzically.

She kept growling. Megs crouched into a position as if she was ready to pounce.

"Megs," I said again, my tone more firm.

Ignoring my warning, Megs sprung! She went straight for Edrick's leg before I could do anything. He shouted in agony as her teeth stink into his calf, blood beginning to seep through the fabric. I scrambled to get a hold of my dog, Will doing the same.

"Megs, no! Let go of his leg!" I ordered above her ravenous snarls.

As I finally grabbed her collar, Will pried her jaws open and off of Edrick's leg. I noticed that not once did Megs try to hurt Will while he forced her mouth agape. Pulling my dog back, I didn't dare loosen my grip on her, but Megs barked loudly at Edrick, straining against my hold.

"Megs, calm down *right* now!" I said sharply. Megs stopped trying to escape my grip and reluctantly went on all fours. The hair on the back of her neck still bristled and she still growled at Edrick.

"I am so sorry, Edrick!" I apologized, "I have no idea what has gotten into her. She's never like this."

"It's fine. Perhaps I smell like chicken." Edrick forced a smile, clutching his left leg.

"The bite marks aren't very deep and aren't fatal," Will said after inspecting the wound.

"That's good," I commented. "Will, why don't you take Edrick to get his leg bandaged? I need to take care of Megs."

"Alright," Will agreed.

I apologized to Edrick again before I dragged my dog away.

I couldn't sleep. Thoughts kept racing through my head, colliding into each other, making my head spin. Worry over John was ever present, but as of now, another pressing matter caught my mind's primary attention.

My suspicions of Edrick hadn't left. How could a man be so calm when hearing about death and destruction? And why was it that the locations in which Akelin's attacks took place had never once stepped foot in Edrick's territory? Could Edrick be a traitor? No, he couldn't. He might not be an incredibly trustworthy guy, but he would never betray the King and join Akelin. Would he?

Putting Akelin aside—which was much harder to do since he'd been our key problem over the past couple weeks—something seemed so off about the knight. Megs could sense something was up with Edrick, too. Perhaps it was a sign. Dogs did have a good opinion on character. I remembered my father using them to hunt for criminals several times in his day. They were almost always successful. Once, a dog stopped an assassination on Sir Levi.

I didn't know how, but the dog must've sensed a dangerous man in its midst.

Edrick was not the man he seemed. I wondered what he was hiding. Or worse, what he's planning.

I awoke with a start as I held up my dagger to the empty air. Timidly setting it aside, I realized I was only dreaming. *He* had been haunting my dreams of late. My hand suddenly went to the still healing scab on my shoulder. My finger traced the mark there as the image of Akelin's face faded away like a ghost in my mind. I didn't know how I knew it was his face, for I had never seen him before, but I knew it was him. I could feel it in my bones.

Hastily, I got dressed and pulled on my boots. Megs looked up at me and whimpered. "It's all right, girl. I'll be back soon. Trust me if I could, I would take you with me. Maybe next time," I soothed, scratching her behind the ears as she reluctantly rested her head on her paws.

Stepping out the door, I closed it quietly and snuck down the hallway past the King and Queen's bedchamber. A jar in the pit of my stomach forced me to realize... Turning around, I slowly crept back to the King and Queen's bedchamber, finding the door open. They never left the door open, not even a crack.

I put my face up to the crack and peered into the room without the risk of being spotted. A candle light in the room helped me to see better in the otherwise darkness. I gasped.

A hooded figure held a sword to King Richard's throat. The King stood beside the bed, his face grave. The Queen was awake, frozen in shock and fear that if she moved, then the imposter would slit her husband's throat. A sense of anger and urgency pounded in my chest. I took the dagger out of my boot, holding it at the ready. Slowly, I pushed the door open, thankful it didn't squeak. I snuck up towards the hooded man.

The Queen spotted me, her eyes widening. I shook my head and put a finger to my lips, indicating to be quiet. She looked away, clearly understanding my message. Thankfully, the King hadn't seen me, or at least didn't indicate that he did. His fierce eyes were fixed on the attacker.

I raised my dagger, ready to strike the imposter. Suddenly, the man whipped around and his sword clashed against my dagger. The hood covered the man's head, a cloth mask concealing half his face, but I saw a smile form on the man's lips as he crooned, "Hello, *Princess*."

I'd heard that voice; it sent chills up my spine. "Hello yourself," I responded between clenched teeth as I shoved him away.

King Richard instantly took the opportunity to grab the blade concealed under his mattress. He whipped back around to face the masked figure, his eyes alight with fervor. The man stepped back, positioning his sword to face both of us.

Looking at my dagger and then back up at me, he chuckled, "What do you expect to do with *that*?"

I realized that I was at a disadvantage, my dagger against this vaguely familiar man's sword. But it was still two to one. I sneered at him, "Stop you."

He laughed, sending another eerie chill up my spine. Logically, my thinking was that the man should surrender now, seeing as he was outnumbered, but he didn't appear to take that into consideration.

In the same instant, before anything could be done, he pulled a knife from his sleeve and threw it in a single motion. The Queen screamed. My world fell away. The hilt protruded from King Richard's core, his face falling as shock and betrayal overwhelmed him. Blood spread over his robes quickly in that instant that went on forever. King Richard fell back, slumping against the edge of the bed as his sword clattered to the floor. Queen Veronica cried out in anguish again, scrambling to her fallen husband.

A rage of white hot anger burned inside of me. Throwing my dagger at the man, the blade grazed his shoulder. I hated that I let my anger throw off my aim, but at least I hit him. It wasn't a graze that caused pain, however, but it did catch his attention.

With him distracted for the moment, I sprinted for the King's fallen sword on the floor. Grasping it, I spun around and positioned myself protectively over the King and Queen, holding my sword in front of me. By now, the man had his sword extended as well.

I lunged at him, slicing his shirt and creating a blood red line across his stomach. The action caused the man to back up. I couldn't help but notice him having a slight limp on his left leg. A bell rang in my mind as I realized who this traitor was.

"Edrick?"

"Guilty as charged." He gave a mocking bow. As he stood up straight again, his hood fell back and he slipped off his cloth mask, revealing Edrick's face and long fair hair.

"You're working for *him*?" I proclaimed, my anger boiling vigorously. "How could you? We trusted you!"

"How could I not? There is no way you can defeat him! He is too powerful. His numbers are many. There is *no* end to the reign of Akelin." He smiled evilly.

I raised my sword and brought it crashing down, intending to send a blow to his head, but Edrick raised his sword to meet mine. The sound of clashing metal rang throughout the room. My sword slid off of his, leaving me vulnerable for the moment. He smacked me in the face with the hilt and my cheek smarted instantly.

"I honestly don't want to hurt you, Princess," his voice dripped with honey. "Join me. Akelin has promised me a good life, keeping my territory and more. We can rule together."

I could hardly believe the audacity of this request! How could he expect me to even consider his offer when my father was dying right behind him? My sword met his. I clashed it again and again, trying to cause some harm to the traitor. My fury only seemed to amuse him. Briefly pushing away my anger to better my control, I swiped my blade to rake across his knuckles, another wound not deep enough to cause fatality to his fingers, unfortunately.

He backed away slightly, dodging a blow that would've rid him of an appendage. As if coming to the realization that I meant him harm, Edrick began advancing. His blade grazed my left forearm, cutting the fabric and leaving a painful line of blood.

Finding myself backing up to the doorway, I tried to advance farther into the room, but Edrick seemed to have other ideas. He pushed me into the hall, thrusting me against the wall. I held up my sword to block his blow. Our swords crossed and pressed against my chest. My knee fought to hit him, but he only used his leg to press up against mine, holding it in place. I looked over the blades and my eyes met Edrick's, which glistened with mischief and playfulness. His smile widened.

"What are you waiting for?" I asked daringly.

"If you expect me to kill you, *Princess*, you are sadly mistaken," he responded, his voice sickly sweet.

"Well then, what *are* you planning to do with me?" I hissed, afraid of the response.

His free hand reached for my wrist. I tensed as his fingers traced the bleeding scrape on my forearm, his touch soft, blood smearing. I didn't like the feel of his thumb, as if he were trying to wipe away the wound. If I could move, I would—as Hugh would say—run my sword strait through him. A small twitch of a smile formed at the edge of his mouth. It made me sick.

Edrick's face leaned towards mine. Panicked, I squirmed to try to get out of his grip, but he didn't do as I expected, his mouth pressing against my ear, his hot breath prickling my neck.

"I will have you as my wife, *Princess*. Akelin has promised this, and I will see that it is so," he whispered smoothly, the words sending a chill of pure, cold hatred up my spine. Edrick paused, his lips brushing my ear before he added softly, "I will not touch you until then."

My breath stopped short, my heart pounding heavily, limbs suddenly stiff. Edrick pulled away slowly, his brown eyes on mine with that strange fixation. Soon, he'd backed away so as I was no longer pressed to the wall. Still, I didn't move. He took a small step, the tenseness in his arms lessening, his guard falling away from my meek appearance.

Energy jolting through my bones and cold anger flowing through my veins, I struck out with my leg, kicking him in the shins. His face instantly screwed up as he groaned. Punching him in the stomach, he doubled over in pain. Using his instability to my advantage, I kicked him away from me and he stumbled back into the King and Queen's bedchamber.

Edrick recollected himself, right before I raised my sword. I breathed heavily, as did he. His sword met mine with a clang, sweeping my blade away, causing it to drop. I didn't bother retrieving it. Balling my fists, I attacked in hand to sword combat, recalling the special training I'd received from Sir Hugh. Knights weren't typically learned in this form of combat, but being a female warrior in a male knight world, Hugh deemed it best for me to have a more forceful advantage, making my lesser strength and better agility bend to my benefit.

I ducked instantly as Edrick's blade whistled over my head. Popping up at once, I swung my leg up and around, kicking him full in the face. Edrick stumbled back, striking out with his sword. The blow sliced my shin due to lack of aim and I cried out as stinging pain shot up the cut.

Ramming myself into his stomach, Edrick fell, his sword clattering to the ground and skidding out of the way. He gasped, the breath knocked out of him. Knowing I was only

160

able to hold him down in his shock, I pounded my fist against his face and punched him in the gut for good measure. As soon as I felt him move to get up, I knocked him in the jaw again, my knuckles no doubt bleeding by then.

With the traitor stunned, I grabbed for my fallen knife which I'd thrown earlier. Clutching it in my fist, I plunged the short blade down towards Edrick's chest. His reflexes were too fast and his hand shot up, grasping my wrist to cut my blow short.

Edrick spat out blood, his face full of frustration and a hint of entertainment. He jabbed his knee into my abdomen, flipping me over to get atop me. His fist collided against my stomach, leaving me gasping for air. Pulling my hair to get my head to face him again, Edrick pried the knife from my fingers and used the hilt to bash me in the side of the head. I cried out in pain, my vision blurring as everything became a slow haze around me.

Vaguely, I heard the barking of a dog and the scratching on wood beyond the ringing in my ears.

Edrick smiled cruelly, raising the knife again. That smile was the last thing I saw before the blow came and darkness overtook me.

I got dressed quickly, thoughts racing, gut tightening upon hearing the commotion upstairs. Bolting for the door, an image of Edrick crossed my mind; hence I turned back and grabbed my sword before heading out the door.

Making my way up the flight of stairs, quickly but quietly, I arrived at the top and came to an abrupt halt. The King and Queen's bedchamber door was open, a light lit inside. A cry in anguish through hysterical weeping sounded in the room. Megs was going crazy in Sam's chamber, her claws audible as she scraped against the door. Drawing my sword, I slinked just outside the room to investigate.

I held my breath, not wanting to make a noise from the sight I saw. The King slumped on the floor, red staining the front of his robes. The Queen knelt beside his limp form, crying in rage and sorrow at another being, her hands pressed against the King's wound. A bloody knife lay beside her.

Following the Queen's furious gaze, my eyes fell on a man rising to his feet as he retrieved a fallen sword. At the ground before him, my heart leaped at the sight of Sam, her form deadly still, her body beaten and bloody.

"How could you?" the Queen screamed at the man. "You killed them!"

"No, Your Ladyship," the man's voice crooned. "I did not kill either one of them, but I'll soon fix that."

The Queen, without once stopping to think in the one moment before I entered, snatched the bloody knife from the ground and was on her feet in an instant. She charged the man, the short blade raised, but the intruder only knocked the dagger from her hand with a single swipe of his blade. She raised her fist to punch him, but the man whacked aside her arm and sent a blow to her face, throwing her to the ground, furious tears staining her cheeks. She lunged for a fallen sword, the hilt almost in her grasp, but the man kicked her in the gut, knocking the breath out of her. The wretch chuckled, placing his foot atop the Queen's outstretched arm and slowly putting his weight on her wrist. She cried out in pain, clawing at his ankle with her good arm and attempting to kick or bite him. He only pressed harder.

I snuck up behind the man, anger compressing my chest, prepared to strike. I didn't know why I thought that sneaking up would do the trick, for there seemed to be no logic in it. At least it bought me enough time to get close to the traitor. The man turned slowly around as if sensing my presence, releasing the Queen from his foot. I could see his face, an evil smile on his lips. I found no shock in my recognition.

"Hello, Will," Edrick greeted. "You don't look too surprised. Did you come to join the party? I know she did." He gestured towards Sam with his sword.

"Edrick," I hissed.

Anger lit inside of me, fanning to flame. I struck before Edrick could react. Pinning him to the wall, I held my sword to his throat. His face never changed.

"What are you going to do?" he questioned. "Slit my throat? No. You don't have it in you."

"Oh, *trust* me. I want more than anything to kill you right now," I said, my voice filled with hatred.

"But you can't," Edrick taunted confidently. "You need me *alive*. You, and your dying King, *need* to know what I know. You know it; else you would have killed me by now."

"And you're just going to give us that information freely, are you? You've proven to be opposing that."

"That's very true," he confessed.

He shoved me away, knocking me off balance. I found my footing and blocked the attack Edrick thrust at me. Metal clashed metal. I held my sword with two hands, blocking the

163

fury Edrick presented. I lunged at him, but he easily stepped away from the sharp blade.

Suddenly, he launched himself in midair, landing on top of me, knocking me to the ground. Our blades crossed, blocking his from injuring my face. He smiled his evil smile at me, his face visible over the blades. I was unable to push him off without potentially causing my own decapitation.

"I am going to enjoy this," he jeered, his mouth dripping with blood.

Out of the corner of my vision, I saw the Queen rising from her daughter's side, sword in hand and a dangerous look in her eye. She was going to try to make a move. Her bravery surprised me, though I shouldn't have been so shocked, seeing how great her daughter's courage was, but as heroic her intentions surely were, the Queen obviously did not possess skill in combat. I couldn't allow her to get hurt should Edrick notice her advances.

Now, I remembered and heard the barking and scratching of the dog in the room next door. I grinned as an idea popped into my head.

"Oh, I bet you would," my voice strained from the weight on my chest, "but I still have a few tricks up my sleeve."

I managed to bring my free hand to my lips and blow, making a sheer whistle. Edrick cocked his head, confused.

The crashing of a snapped doorknob filled the hall. Edrick and I turned our heads to the doorway. Standing there with teeth bared and hair standing on end was a fuming Megs, her growl rippling through her entire body. In a way, she shook with anger.

I looked into Edrick's shocked face. "You remember Megs, don't you?"

He stared at me in sheer anger. I could tell he was unnerved by the dog, but not so much that he got petrified. Edrick wrestled to get his blade at my throat, his intentions suddenly clear. He meant to dispatch me first before he went for the dog. That could be my advantage.

"Get him, Megs!" I ordered.

The dog gladly obeyed and leaped through the air, colliding with Edrick and knocking him off of me. She sank her fangs deep into his right arm, his sword dropping with a clank. Edrick screamed in pain. He tried to shake the dog off, but the German Shepherd was too heavy and her hold too set for her to be shaken off so easily.

Standing slowly, I pressed my sword against Edrick's chest. I raised my elbow at an angle, positioning myself so that if Edrick moved in any way towards me, his weapon, or the dog, he'd end up with an instant blade in his chest.

"Shall I tell her to release?" I asked, not bothering to add that I didn't know if the dog would obey me again. "Are you going to cooperate, or should I just let her continue to shred you to bits? Cause honestly, I would prefer the latter option."

He gave another yell in agony and frustration. Megs growled and shook Edrick's arm. The Queen was suddenly right behind the traitor, the end of her blade digging into his back, assuring the indefinite inability to escape. Edrick looked at me and grit his teeth, his eyes burning with hatred and fury.

"It's your choice," I said.

"Release her, and I'll cooperate how I can," he sneered between clenched teeth.

"Alright." I shrugged. "Megs, that's enough."

Megs let go reluctantly. She crawled back to me, never turning her back on Edrick. Her brown eyes looked up, panting and wagging her tail. I patted her on the head, thankful that the dog trusted me enough to obey me.

Edrick moved a little, Megs instantly turning to him and growling again, the Queen holding her stance more rigid. Edrick held out his good hand in defense, as if the mere gesture would stop the dog, but if Megs did decide to attack again, it'd take a lot more than that to save him.

Keeping my sword at his chest, I said coolly, "Now, you are going to do *exactly* as we say."

Chapter Seventeen

I opened my eyes. My head was throbbing. Raising my hands, I found that my knuckles were once again bandaged. Blue and purple bruises peaked out from behind the wrapping, the side effects of using my fists as weapons. My forearm was bound as well, and my shin felt as if it had been tended to also. I could feel the bruises on my body, no need to see them to know they were there. Reaching up, I felt the lump on the side of my head, the pain stinging at the touch. I wasn't dead. That was good.

I sat up, realizing that I still wore the ruined clothes from last night. Was it last night? I didn't know. It could have been a week ago for all I knew. It was all a blur. The time between the event with Edrick and now was just total blackness. I didn't even think I dreamed.

I wondered what happened between then and now. Did the King survive? Did Edrick kill the Queen, too? Did Edrick win? Was I a prisoner? Did someone come and defeat Edrick? If so, who?

So many questions filled my head that it made the headache worse. First things first: I needed to know what happened. I got up and—after briefly wondering how they got there—dress in the clothes laid out on the bed: a simple brown dress with a kind of rope sash that draped down the front. I would've preferred some of my normal clothes, but I supposed this would have to do for now. Besides, the skirt allowed my leg not to be confined. I ignored the petticoats and headed for the door.

Reaching for the handle, my hand froze. Why was the doorknob new? What if it was a trap? What if the door was locked? Both of which would not be good and would mean I really was a prisoner.

I finally just bit my lip and grabbed the handle. It turned, so at least I wasn't locked in my own bedroom. I opened the door and peered outside. It didn't appear to be a trap. I let out a breath and opened it wider, coming out as I did so.

I walked down the passage, my eyes flicking to the King and Queen's bedchamber. The door was closed. When I tried the handle, I found it locked. I didn't see anyone yet, so everyone must've been busy. I quickened my pace, starting to wonder if I was all alone in this great castle. Everything seemed terribly quiet, and it scared me. I slowed down, for the sting in my leg prohibited me from a fast and steady gait. Forced to a limp, I turned the corner and made my way down the stairs as quickly as I could.

At this level, I finally spotted inhabitants. This was the floor where we kept our guests and survivors from the attack on Will's territory. They were doing much better now, but they still needed a place to stay, so they were here until we found somewhere else for them to go. I walked through, trying not to draw much attention to myself though I was sure that I was an atrocious sight to see.

Passing by an open room, my gaze fell on a familiar face and I gave a sigh of relief, "Millie."

My friend turned my way, dropping her sewing. She gasped in shock at the sight of me, affirming my previous thought of my state. Without a word, she rushed to me and embraced me gently.

"Oh, Sam." Millie shook her head. "I heard what happened last night. I can't tell you how relieved I am to see you! You look so much better than I had imagined—still bad, but at least not as bad."

"Thanks." I smiled, though my cheek hurt. "It's good to see you, too."

"But what are you doing here?" Millie questioned, her face full of concern. "Shouldn't you be resting? You shouldn't be up and about in the state you're in."

"No, I'm fine," I insisted, though it wasn't entirely true. "I need to know. Have you heard anything about the King? Is he all right? I don't know what happened after…"

"Hush, you're getting yourself all worked up!" Millie scolded. "Yes, the King is all right. He's not exactly *good*, being stabbed in the stomach and all, but the physician says he'll survive. The knife didn't damage any organs or arteries, which is lucky."

I sighed in relief. The King was all right. That was the best news I'd heard in a long while. In the back of my mind, I knew that the throw wasn't luck at all. Edrick was an expert knife-thrower. I'd seen him in action before at tournaments, and he was renowned for his aim. Why did Edrick not kill the King when he had the chance? Did he want to revel in the kill later? Or was it my presence that threw off his plans? Millie continued on with what she knew, so I tuned in to pay attention.

"Who would have thought Sir Edrick was a traitor? It's terrible, isn't it?" Millie went on. "At least Sir William made it there in time. Otherwise, who knows what would have happened?"

"Will killed Edrick?" I questioned.

"Well, he didn't kill him," Millie admitted, "but he stopped him, and I heard that your dog had something to do with it, too. That could just be some rumors, though."

"Where's Will?"

"The King called the Great Knights to interrogate the traitor," Millie responded. "They are going to get information out of him before Edrick is sent to the dungeons until his hanging."

I nodded. "I should go. Thank you, Millie."

"Let me help you." Millie skittered after me.

I shook my head. "No, Millie. Besides, you can't come, you know that." I squeezed her hand. "I'm fine, don't worry."

"No, you're not, but you're too stubborn to admit it," she sighed. "Fine, but take it easy, Sam. You shouldn't push yourself so much."

I only nodded as I limped away. I had a feeling I knew exactly where they were interrogating Edrick, and as much as I shuddered at the thought of seeing him again, I knew that I needed to do this. I needed to know what he had to say just as much as anyone else.

I was on my way to see Edrick, who was locked in a windowless room with two guards watching the door from the outside and two watching the traitor on the inside. Hugh, Levi, myself and Sam—once she's recovered—were to check on him every two hours or so. He should be unable to even get close to escaping. Right now, Hugh, Levi and I were going to interrogate him.

As I walked down the hall, my vision went blurry and my head started to hurt all of a sudden. I must've just been getting a little headache from lack of sleep last night. I leaned against the wall for a moment until I could see clearly again and the place behind my eyes stopped throbbing. It was a long night and I must've been tired more than I thought. I sighed, rubbing my temples.

Passing a hand over my face in a failed attempt to brush away the fatigue, I opened my eyes and gave a start. Sam stood right in front of me, her face expressing concern. I almost laughed. I was probably the last person she should've been concerned about.

"Will?" She stepped closer to me, her hand on my shoulder. "Are you all right?"

"Uh-huh," I groaned.

Sam pushed a strand of hair behind her ear. I examined her thoughtfully, checking to see if she was all right. She hadn't healed overnight, that's for sure, but at least she was alive. That's what was most important.

My eyes fell on the bandages on her hands. Hopefully I patched her up correctly. As she hadn't been fatally injured, she didn't get instant treatment. The physician was too focused on helping the King as he should have been. Seeing as Sam was hurt, I took it in my own hands to bind her

171

wounds—with the help of another servant, of course. The Queen came in, too, a few times, just to check up on Sam. I was just glad she was better.

"What happened after I went out?" Sam asked. "Millie said you were there."

"He didn't kill them if that's what you're asking," I informed. "And it wasn't really *me* who got Edrick. It was actually Megs. She has good instincts. What happened to you before you blacked out?"

"Um," she started rubbing her bandaged arm and looked away, "he... he just... he had the upper hand, that's all."

I knew there was more to what she was saying, more than she let on. Whatever happened, I hated Edrick for it. I hated him for making Sam uncomfortable, for beating her, for hurting her. I hated him for all the damage he'd done, for all the pain he'd caused in such a short amount of time, for being a traitor to his King and country.

Sam looked into my eyes. "Take me to him."

I decided to keep what happened last night a secret. I didn't want to have to discuss it with anyone, for I was still trying to make sense of it. I didn't have *any* feelings for Edrick, and even if I had before yesterday, they were defiantly gone now. What bothered me most was that I hadn't even suspected him to be a traitor.

I knew now how Akelin knew about our meeting at the Golden Rose, and I knew now that I wasn't supposed to be there. They didn't *expect* me to be there! Otherwise the King would be dead and Akelin would probably be in control of Etheland. I was the one who spoiled they're plans. I just wondered why I wasn't dead. I think I knew, for Edrick showed me that last night. I just didn't want to admit it.

Will interrupted my thoughts, "We're here."

The door was guarded by two soldiers. A shiver traveled down my spine. I knew that Edrick knew I was here. Even though I couldn't see him, I could feel his eyes. They were watching me, sensing my every movement. My blood ran cold and another chill went up my spine.

"You don't have to do this," Will said softly.

He reached out and touched my arm. The heat from his hand spread over my arm and made me feel warm again. I shook my head. "Yes, I do."

He nodded as he pulled back his hand. The warmth lingered, though. A guard opened the door. I took a deep breath before I walked into the room, followed by Will. Brown eyes looked up at me, wickedness dancing behind them.

My blood went cold again as the sickly sweet words escaped his lips, "Hello, *Princess*."

Sam froze as if unable to move, unable to speak. She acted like she had right before she told me what happened to her parents: haunted, trapped in a nightmare. I took her by the arm and led her to the wall. She seemed to snap out of it, nodding in thanks. I nodded back.

Hugh was already here, giving Edrick the stare down. I could tell all he wanted to do was punch the traitor in the face, but was reluctantly holding his wrath back. Levi was here as well, though he hid his anger better than Hugh. I was glad he was here.

Edrick smiled cruelly at me. I kept my face stone cold despite the loath raving inside.

Levi said in a cool, deadly tone, "You know how this goes, Edrick. Tell us what we need to know, and you can have a faster execution. It's more than you deserve."

Edrick smiled. "Well, this all depends on what you need to know."

"And don't start lying to us either!" Hugh warned angrily. "No more tricks and no more lies!"

"Now, Hugh! With that attitude, you won't get anywhere," Edrick said icily.

Hugh looked like he was about to explode! Somehow, he held it in as he turned to Levi and asked, "Might I knock something into 'im?"

"Be my guest." Levi shrugged.

Hugh immediately made a fist and punched Edrick in the gut. Edrick groaned and doubled over from the impact.

He looked up, still smiling. "Is that all you've got, dwarf?"

Hugh muttered something and raised his fist to send another blow. "I'll show you all I've got," he grumbled.

"That's enough, Hugh," Levi stated. "We can't have him dying just yet. He still has an execution to attend."

Hugh reluctantly lowered his fist, scowling at the traitor sitting before him. Edrick just stared right back with mischief and cruelty. I looked back at Sam, who hadn't said

174

a word since she stepped through the door. She stared at her folded, bandaged hands, pondering something. What was troubling her?

"Where is Akelin?" I asked, averting my attention back to Edrick.

"If you expect me to know, you are quite mistaken," he responded, his voice smooth as butter.

"He's lying," Hugh accused.

Edrick laughed, "You would think so, but sadly no. I am not lying. I have no clue where he is right now."

"What do you mean that you don't know where he is?" I questioned, thinking that now I was the one about to burst.

Edrick stood up, the chains binding his hands to the floor stretching as far as they could, looking right at me. "Just as it sounds. After I killed the King, I was going to inform Akelin the good news. If I wasn't there by this morning, they were to change location. Since I didn't come, they would have moved. You will never find him."

"How great are the troops?" Levi asked, his voice gravelly and foreboding.

"Getting bigger every day. We have more men than you all have combined," Edrick said confidently.

That was it! Before the blink of an eye, I rushed up to Edrick and threw him up against the wall. He didn't even bother to struggle to get out of my grip. "What did he promise you?" I growled, "What did Akelin promise you so that you would turn against the King?"

His eyes moved away from mine, looking behind me. I followed his gaze and I swore that if I wasn't authorized otherwise, I would've strangle him right here, right now.

I pinned him harder against the wall and said so only Edrick could hear, "You will *never* have her. Not as long as I'm alive."

Edrick's eyes glimmered. "That can be arranged."

"William, that's enough," Levi said behind me.

I reluctantly released Edrick and backed away. Hugh clapped me on the back, which surprised me because I didn't know he could reach my shoulder. Edrick looked at me mockingly as he straightened his shirt.

"We must go now," Levi stated. "Guards, take this brute to the dungeons."

Levi exited the room, whilst Hugh and I followed in suit as the guards entered. As I left, I heard Sam ask Edrick, "Why didn't you kill me last night?"

"Oh, Princess," I heard the silky voice answer her, "you know why."

Chapter Eighteen

Try as I might, I couldn't get Edrick's words out of my head. I wanted to forget, I really did, but it was harder than expected. The thing was, when something like what happened last night occurred, all I wanted to do was forget it. It was impossible, though, because a little part of me *wanted* to think about it, make sense of it, and pretty soon that little part of me got so big that it filled my mind and it was all I could think about. Sometimes, something broke through the confusion and made me realize what was going on. It woke up my mind. That was what happened now—the something that woke up my muddled up brain was Will.

Well, not exactly. I didn't think he meant to, but it couldn't be helped. All he did was take my hand to make sure I was all right. Nothing big or special. I didn't even know why this woke me from my pondering, but as I thought before, it couldn't be helped. I shoved the confusing fog of thoughts to the back of my mind and looked up into Will's green eyes.

I gave a little smile to him, and he smiled back. Following him to a room where Hugh already set up a map and was conversing something with Levi and… My breath caught in my throat as I found the King lying on a long couch propped up on a pile of pillows. His hand rested on his abdomen where the knife wound lay beneath a thick lump of bandages. Face pale, but he was alive. Will released my hand as we joined them.

"What are we going to do?" Will asked King Richard. "Now that we know Edrick's men are with Akelin, we have lost a considerable amount of soldiers and scouts."

"That is what we were just discussing," the King answered, his voice strained, "but I think I have an idea."

"What is this idea?" Hugh asked.

Something in my head clicked. "The Secret Woods," I said so softly it could only be described as a whisper.

"What?" Will turned to me quizzically.

I looked up at the four men before me. "The Secret Woods: Robin's Woods."

King Richard nodded his head at me, shifting slightly on the couch. "Yes, precisely. We must ask for aid from Robin of the Secret Woods."

Will's eyes widened with astonishment. "Are you sure there is no other way?" he was almost pleading in his tone.

"Yes, it is our only hope," King Richard said. "We need more men and Akelin will not expect this."

"But the Secret Woods is a sanctuary for those who need someplace to stay," Will continued. "It is a place for the homeless, not warriors."

"That might have been the original intentions," Levi spoke up, "but you know as well as I that Robin has made it much more than that."

Confused by his reaction, I asked Will, "What is wrong with you and Robin of the Secret Woods?"

Looking me in the eyes, there was something in them that revealed he didn't enjoy talking about this. "He's my brother."

Brother? Frozen in place, my tongue seemed not to work anymore. Robin of the Secret Woods was Will's brother?

"What!" Hugh sputtered before I could say anything. "That pilfering forest dweller is *your filthy brother*?" He jabbed a finger at Will's chest.

Levi stepped forward with a fixed expression, "Yes, he is. And that *pilfering forest dweller* is the son of a war hero and former Great Knight... and my friend." His face darkened slightly, "And that pilfering forest dweller is about to turn the tables of this war."

Hugh grunted, acknowledging the end of the discussion. But that didn't stop my question from nagging my mind: why didn't Will tell me?

Walking with Sam, I didn't wish to utter a word. I knew that Robin and his band may be our only chance of overcoming Akelin, but I didn't want to face him, not yet. Some might've thought I would wish to see my own brother after not seeing him in seven years, but no, I didn't. I'd heard the stories of Robin of the Secret Woods. I was somewhat happy for him, and I guess it wasn't exactly that I didn't want to see him. It was just hard. My own brother left me for no good reason, so that gave me a right to be apprehensive about meeting him again. Right?

Sam said something that interrupted my thoughts, the whisper probably more for herself than for me. "What?" I asked her.

"Your brother?" she said again. "Why didn't you tell me you had a brother? I mean, you know about my past, and now I realize, I don't know much about yours."

I sighed, "I've just tried so hard to forget about it."

"I have more reason to try to forget my past than anyone else!" Sam fired back.

"Look, I don't know, alright? I don't *think* about Robin all that much. He left after our father died and wasn't there when Mother got sick and died as well. I know little about him, now. Frankly, I don't exactly *wish* to see him again."

"But that's just it," Sam said softly. "I still don't understand how you cannot want to see your own brother again. Who cares what he did, he's your brother. I would give *anything* to see my sister again!"

"Well…" I was running out of come-backs. "I don't know if he wants to see me again."

"Is that the best you can come up with?" Sam shot. With a controlled sigh, she seemed to contain her frustration, her next words coming out in a dangerous even tone, "Look, tomorrow you and I are heading out to the Secret Woods to negotiate with your brother. If there are any feuds still between you two, try to behave. We're not going there to fight or to bring up any old quarrels—or new ones. Alright?"

I nodded. Sam turned around with a swish of skirts and whisked off. As I continued to walk down the hall, thoughts raced through my mind. I really hadn't shared my past with Sam, and I knew a lot about hers. I should open up a little bit more to her.

My mind pondered over the conversation I only recently witnessed. It was before Will and I left when I was going about through the castle. I happened upon the King and Queen in a bit of an argument or a passionate conversation. I wouldn't have minded. I would have just continued on, for their disagreements were never all that heated; this time though, they were talking about me. In fact, they were almost *arguing* about me. Their words kept running through my head:

"No, I forbid it!" Queen Veronica had exclaimed. *"I won't have my daughter go off anymore for anything that has to do with this war!"*

"I wouldn't have her do it if it weren't that I need her," King Richard persisted. *"She's one of the best knights I've got. In fact, Samantha is the only knight I can fully trust at this point! She is also a Great Knight, and with that comes certain duties and responsibilities to the kingdom."*

"But she shouldn't be out there," Queen Veronica argued. *"She'll only get herself killed!"*

"She has a good head on her shoulders and an even better skill with both sword and speech than anyone I know, never mind her being a girl," the King went on. *"She has less of a chance of getting herself killed than anyone else."*

"Samantha needs to stay here," the Queen's voice was pleading then. *"She needs to learn the ways of a lady. If she is to be Etheland's Queen someday, she must know how to be a proper one!"*

"And if she is to be a ruler, then she must know how to do such!" King Richard countered, his voice growing softer. *"I know that she is your daughter and you want what is best and safest for her, but she is also my daughter, and I cannot do this without her. One day, we will no longer be here to guide her and shelter her. One day, Samantha will be Queen, and she must be prepared for any and all situations to which a great and noble ruler must face."*

"I just don't want her to end up dead, whether it be in the midst of a battlefield or at the hand of a traitor," the Queen spoke softly.

"I know," the King comforted. *"Neither do I."*

I left then, not wishing to be caught eavesdropping, but the words continued to penetrate me still. I never thought of being Queen before. I always figured—being an adopted princess—that this was an honor forbidden to me. I never comprehended that on the day I was accepted into the royal family, I became the heir to the throne. It was a new feeling, a strange surprise, to know that I would someday be Queen. It'd become almost a new fear as well.

I was more than grateful that the King trusted me so much that he would be so forthcoming in arguing on my behalf though I knew that the Queen also had the best of intentions. It brought tears to my eyes when I tried to think how much they really loved me. To think, they called me daughter. They'd always called me that, of course, but I'd always been present when they did. It's different knowing that they still thought of me as their daughter—an honest and true one—even when they were discussing amongst themselves alone.

Suddenly noticing my lack in pace, I snapped out of the depths of my mind, urging Autumn to ride faster. Catching up with Will, we continued riding for the Secret Woods.

We'd packed lightly for the trip, for we didn't know how long we would be gone. Will and I were each armed with both sword and bow. Autumn and Billy ran swiftly and surely over the hills and through the towns. Will and I had not talked much since yesterday. We'd been a little too busy for talking.

The rumors of Robin ran through my mind. The forest *before* Robin came was supposedly haunted. When Robin arrived, he started a new reputation for the area. Though anyone who went into the woods hardly ever came out. Thus started the tales of Robin of the Secret Woods. It was amazing how fast stories could spread over so little time.

Autumn slowed down to a walk as we entered the forest. The trees were so thick, only little streams of light could make it through. Oddly quiet here, I pulled the hood of my cape up over my head, covering my braided hair and causing a shadow to fall over my face.

The silence screamed in my ears. Neither the twitter of a bird in song, nor the scampering of tiny paws could be heard. The sun hitting the leaves of the trees cast a greenish glow in the woods. The only sounds—though would have been so soft but were pounding against my ears—were the horses' hooves falling on the ground in a rhythmic walk, the steady breathing the four of us made, and the beating of my heart.

I finally managed to ask softly, "How will we find him?"

"Find him? No, we won't find him. *He* will find *us*," Will answered mysteriously. "If, for whatever reason, he doesn't, I think I can remember the way."

The only thing that was comforting me about meeting this Robin was the fact that he was Will's brother. Otherwise, I might not have been here by choice. I had to admit, it was rather exciting.

"How old is your brother anyway?" I asked, trying to break the silence.

"He's about twenty-two now," he replied.

"Oh," I said, unsure how to respond. I honestly wanted to hear more about Will's relationship with Robin, their time growing up together, how the whole *Robin of the Secret Woods* started, but Will didn't seem to want to talk about it, at least not yet. I'd find a way to wrestle the truth out of him.

"How are we going to go about the negotiations?" I questioned. "He's your brother. What is he most likely to respond to?"

Will didn't take long to answer, "I hate to say it, but it might have to be you he'll respond better to."

"Me? Why?"

"Just," he paused, as if trying to find the right words, "keep him *intrigued*."

"Well, how am I supposed to do that?" I asked, still not quite understanding what he wanted me to do.

"Robin is playful," Will admitted. "Always has been, always will be. He'll be very much interested in the fact that you're a knight, so, if you make him interested, he'll let us stay."

I nodded, suddenly not so thrilled to meet Robin as I might have been before. Keep him intrigued? I supposed I could do that.

Will and I continued to keep our horses at a walk through the woods. The snap of a tree branch echoed through the stillness and quiet. Suddenly, we found ourselves surrounded! Thirty men or so had their bows drawn and their arrows at the ready. I pulled on Autumn's reigns, causing her to stop.

A man called out to us, "What is your business here?"

"We are here to see Robin of the Secret Woods," I stated boldly.

Someone snickered. If it wasn't for the hood covering my face and hair, these men would probably have a riot.

"Get off of your horses and drop your weapons on the ground," the man ordered.

I slipped off Autumn and hesitated before I lowered my bow and quiver on the ground before me. I took off my sheathed sword, seeing Will doing the same. A man came up to gather the weapons.

"Now put your hands behind your backs," the man called out again.

Reluctantly, I did as he said. The cuts and scrapes on my knuckles burned slightly as someone roughly took them to tie my wrists together. Someone else did the same to Will. The men lowered their arrows seeing that we are defenseless.

The man who'd spoken earlier smiled now as he gave a sharp whistle. A small horse-drawn covered wagon came rattling out of the woods. Autumn and Billy were tied to the wagon and Will and I were told to get in the back.

The man sneered at us as he said, "Welcome to the Secret Woods, gentlemen."

Chapter Nineteen

Though we were already close, I leaned over to Sam. "I don't think this is such a good idea."

"Would you relax? It's not that bad," she protested.

"Really? Our hands are bound, our weapons are gone, and we're in the back of a wagon going who knows where," I said this though I knew exactly where we're going. I had been there before. In fact, I helped build it.

"Who says my hands are bound?" Sam asked slyly.

"What do you mean?" I asked, confused.

Sam took her bandaged hands from behind her back, the rope in one of them. I looked at her in awe. A smile formed under the shadow of her hood. "A little trick I learned on the streets," she explained. She put her hands back behind her back, pretending she was still tied up.

I shook my head. "Also, what are they going to do when they find out that you're a girl? The Princess nonetheless!"

"I can take care of myself, thank you very much. Besides, he's your brother! Why are *you* the one asking all these questions?"

"A brother I haven't seen in *seven years*! Who knows how much he's changed since last I saw him? He's almost like an outlaw. How are we supposed to trust him?"

The driver yelled back at us, "Hey, keep it down! No talking!"

Sam leaned close enough for me to see her face under her hood and feel her breath on my skin, her leg pressed against mine. She whispered, "First of all, Robin is not an outlaw."

"He's close enough," I stated. Robin had committed enough crimes to be an outlaw. He'd just never been caught, never had any proof it was him. At least he wasn't a murderer or a traitor or done any other violent or physical actions against the law… that I knew of.

Sam ignored my comment. "Second of all, I don't care if we're *supposed to trust him*. I hardly trust anyone right now, but we need the extra men. We need Robin and his group on our side. Otherwise, Akelin is going to win and cause even more darkness and fear to spread throughout Etheland. There is no option. We must do this, or all could be lost."

I nodded, understanding the truth in what she said. I still couldn't help but feel reluctant. To this day, I hadn't forgiven Robin for what he did. He abandoned us! He abandoned our mother and it broke her heart. He left me to see everything fall apart in his wake. How could he have caused so much good by causing so much pain?

After about ten more minutes of being jostled about from the bumpy road, the wagon finally stopped. "Welcome to the Secret Village," the wagon driver laughed.

I looked into Sam's eyes and she looked into mine. She gave a nod as she pulled her hood lower over her face. I let out a sigh before we were let out of the wagon.

The Secret Village. I had only heard stories about this place, and now I was actually here. Wait until Owen and Isabel heard about this! The village was bigger than I'd thought. The houses—huts are more like it—are simple with mud or wood walls and roofs of branches or straw. Not only were men here, but women and children as well. A stable and a blacksmith's shop stood amongst the dwellings; it was really an actual village. Who would have thought?

When I looked to Will to see his reaction, he gazed around like he'd seen it before. Of course, I should have expected he'd been here already, being Robin's brother and all. I supposed I just thought that the boys' feud started before the Secret Woods.

I wondered how long this place had been around here for. Perhaps the stories only came a long while after its existence? I added this to the ever growing list of questions to ask Will later.

The two of us were led on, entering the village but not getting too deeply into it. One of the men shouted, "Hey, Robin! Look what we found wandering in our woods."

A young man started walking toward us. I could tell he was Will's brother the moment I laid eyes on him. He had the same brown hair as Will, though a little longer. He was tall and handsome, I hated to admit. His eyes weren't green like Will's. More like a hazel color since they seemed to change from green to brown to almost a blue. Robin appeared to be the kind of man who was carefree and liked to have fun. He may have had just a touch of vanity about him.

Robin smiled mischievously. "Now, who is this?"

Someone caused Will and me to get down on our knees. My hood still covered my face with a shadow, causing me not to see above my head. I relied on my ears to know what was going on.

"Will?" I heard Robin question. "Is that really you, brother?"

"Hello, Robin," Will responded.

I heard laughing. "How long has it been? Two, three years?" Robin asked.

"It's been seven years," Will said in the same low voice that sounded almost dangerous.

"Seven years? It's really been that long? Hmm..." Robin said to himself. I thought he'd forgotten I was still here. I continued not to say anything, for I didn't know what would happen if I did. Robin continued, "And how is Mother doing?"

Will answered softly, "She's dead."

A pause went on before Robin grunted, as if forcing the question out, "When did she die?"

"Four months after you left." Again, I heard the dangerous tone in Will's voice.

"Well, this is terrible news," Robin's voice sounded as if it were attempting to be strong, trying to brush off the news by hiding any sorrows behind a mask that seemed as if he did not care at all. "But we must move on."

I heard Will mutter something very quietly under his breath. Robin knelt on one knee, resting his elbow on the other, in front of me. "Now who do we have here?" he questioned, mischief in his voice.

Suddenly, Robin whipped back my cape's hood. My braided red hair fell over my shoulder. I looked up into his hazel eyes. He looked shocked, but clearly intrigued. There had been plenty of different reactions to finding out my gender. This one was not new to me.

A smile appeared on his face. "And who might you be, may I ask?"

"I go by many names," I answered, keeping in mind Will's advice to intrigue. "Samantha Lionton is my birth name, everyone calls me Sam. Most know me as Sam the Lion Heart." I left out the fact that I was the Princess.

"So *you* are the famous Sam the Lion Heart. This is quite a surprise," Robin said. "And what name am I to call you, pray tell?"

"Sam; nothing more and nothing less," I responded.

Standing up, Robin stated, "Will, I appreciate the visit, but unless this is all you're here for, you might as well be leaving." He looked at me. "Your girlfriend can stay, though."

Before anyone could stop me—including myself—I pulled out the dagger hidden in my boot and had Robin pinned to the wall, knife at his throat. "First of all, I am not his girlfriend. Second of all, we are not here for a *visit,* we are here to negotiate in the name of the King," I said between clenched teeth.

"Well in that case," Robin raised an eyebrow.

I release him from my grip. I thought I'd found out how to intrigue him, now. Robin thought that this act of violence was entertaining, or little annoyed outbursts at least. He found cunning in a woman interesting. I could do that. Will stood up behind me.

Robin looked me over. "I'm impressed, you managed to get out of your bonds and you managed to fool my men into thinking you're a man. If the negotiations include you staying here in the Secret Woods, whatever it is, I agree."

Almost to test my theory, I threw my dagger at him so that it streaked past Robin's right ear and embedded itself in the wall behind him. The dagger only nicked his ear, so there was nothing serious about that. If anything, Robin just looked more impressed. I thought I was right about him.

"I know it was a joke," I admitted, keeping my face solemn. "Next time, I'll aim just a little more to the left."

Robin nodded, smiling. "You two, follow me."

Will and I did as he said. I couldn't help but think that the two brothers were more alike than they thought; they both knew how to get on my nerves.

Sam and I followed Robin into a nearby hut. He hadn't changed much at all since last I saw him. He was still the arrogant, mischievous, carefree little brother who left years ago.

I felt a tinge of anger every time he looked at Sam in his impressed kind of way. I got that he would be impressed with her. Who wouldn't? It was just the playfulness lurking behind his eyes that gave me the urge to punch him in the face! I regretted telling Sam to keep him intrigued. I was afraid it might have worked too well, even if it was only a few actions. I envied her in the sense that she got to throw a knife at my brother.

Robin turned and offered to Sam, "Please, have a seat." The silky charm in his voice made me cringe.

"Thank you, but I think I'll stand," she responded. I could tell by the tone of her voice that she wasn't in the mood for games or mock hospitality.

"As you wish," Robin said, clearly studying her every move and every word. "Now, what brings you to my woods?"

"A proposal," Sam responded. "We are in need of your help. Are you familiar with the villain, Akelin?"

"I cannot say I know him personally, but yes, I am aware of him."

"Are you aware of his return?"

"No. I have not heard of it."

"He has declared war on King Richard and has caused turmoil in some parts of Etheland."

"What does this have to do with me?"

"He has declared war on the *entire* kingdom, Robin," I said harshly, "that includes you. We've come to ask for you to join forces with the King."

"How do you know that Akelin will come into my woods?" he asked, aggravating me terribly.

"We know because if Akelin takes the throne, he will not want any threat against him," I explained. "That means you and your town. He is not going to take *any* chances! He will come and he will destroy everything and everyone! There would be no escape from that fate."

Robin sat in a chair with a sigh. He folded his hands and put them to his lips, looking from me to Sam repetitively. This was his way of thinking things over. It agitated me.

Bringing his hands to his lap, he asked, "And what, might I ask, are you offering if I join forces with King Richard?"

Sam responded, "You will receive fifty pounds worth of gold…"

"No," Robin interrupted, "Money is no good for me."

"What of land?" Sam asked.

"Why would I need it? I already have all the land I need!"

Sam sighed, "The feeling of happiness and joy in your heart once Akelin is defeated?"

Robin laughed, "Is this all you've got?"

"Glory! You will have the whole kingdom praising you and telling stories about you. They will say how you helped to save Etheland from disaster when all hope was lost. You will be a hero to everyone. Your enemies will be frightened at your very name," I exclaimed, tempting him. "Fame and glory; that is what you want."

A smile spread over Robin's face. "Now, that sounds appealing."

I smirked to myself. I knew this was what he wanted. He had always held praise and glory higher than anything else. Robin loved recognition, good or bad. His conceit had seemed to win the upper hand in almost every situation. This was right up his alley.

"Do we have an agreement?" Sam asked stiffly.

"I believe we do," Robin answered calmly. "You don't have to go, yet, do you? Stay and help prepare for our little adventure."

"We must inform the King," Sam started.

"Really, I insist." Robin stood up while talking. "I will send someone to deliver the message to the King. It is no trouble."

She didn't respond immediately. I could tell that she was pondering this over in her mind. She didn't want to ruin the agreement Robin had just agreed to. I didn't say anything, leaving the decision to her.

Sam looked up and responded, "Alright, but not for too long. We would like to see your troops, how you fight. Not too much fun and games."

"Excellent," Robin declared. "Today, you will see the beauty of my village! Tonight, we shall have a feast to celebrate the alliance between King Richard and myself!"

Chapter Twenty

One of Robin's men left to deliver the message to the King, telling of Robin's agreement to our proposal and that Will and I shall be staying to help prepare. Another of the men led Will and me to an empty hut, the one he said was used for guests. I didn't think they used it much. They didn't receive many guests all that often. I was not happy about having to share a room with Will. I thought he was a little uncomfortable, too, but we solved the problem by mentally dividing the room in half.

Will left the hut so I could get ready for the feast, for both of us got a little dirty on the ride here. After I cleaned myself in the wash basin, I slipped my chain back on around my neck and fingered my ring.

Rummaging around in my bag for clothes, what I found took me by surprise. All the clothes I'd packed for the trip were gone! In their place were a few simple dresses. I rolled my eyes, knowing *exactly* who made the switch. Queen Veronica. I put on a light brown dress with sleeves that ended at the elbows and a blue sash draped in the front. I didn't loathe dresses. I just got so used to wearing men's clothes when I was on the streets that dresses became unnatural to wear. Sometimes they could be comfortable. I quickly brushed my hair and stepped outside.

Will looked at me and cocked an eyebrow. "The Queen," I told him.

"Ah," he responded, knowing her disapproval of my typical wardrobe. He smiled at me before he disappeared inside the guest hut to get ready himself.

I decided to take a look around the village. My eyes closed as I inhaled the scent of the forest. I could live in a place like this. Then again, I *did* live in a place like this, but that was long ago. Starting to walk down the dirt road, the earth felt cool under my bare feet. Smiling at the people I passed, they smiled and nodded in return. A group of kids played ahead of me, compelling me to approach closer to take a better look.

One girl, not much older than Isabel, spied me. I welcomed her with a smile and she bashfully smiled back and slowly started to walk toward me. Staying where I was, I waited for her as she approached, crouching down to look her in the eye.

"Hello," I greeted.

"Hello," she answered.

"My name's Sam, what's yours?"

"Abby," she said shyly. "Is it true that you are really one of the King's Knights?"

Nodding slightly, I responded, "Yes, it is."

"But I thought girls couldn't be knights."

"Well, the King made an exception."

"But you look more like a princess than a knight," Abby admitted.

I laughed, "Well, that is more or less true."

"Why are you here?" she asked.

I sighed, not wanting to say something that might scare her. "I have heard much about the Secret Woods. I wanted to come and see what it's like for myself."

Satisfied with the answer, Abby turned around and returned to the group of kids. I stood up, and before I continued to walk on, someone behind me said, "There you are!"

I turned around and found myself face to face with Robin. I took a step back. "You were looking for me?"

"Well, not exactly," he admitted. "Call it a happy coincidence."

He looked behind me and I followed his gaze. The group of kids were heading this way. Abby came up to me and said, "Some of the boys want to see what you can do. They don't think a girl is quite as good as a boy at being a knight. They didn't believe me when I told them that you're one of the King's Knights. Would you show them?"

I cocked an eye brow. "Well, I'll need my weapons."

"No problem," Robin stated. He smiled at me, a gleam in his eye, "Besides, I'd like to see this for myself."

Leaving the hut in my clean clothes, I couldn't help but look around the town with interest. It had not changed much. It'd grown bigger, much bigger; more people too. Who would have thought that the plan would be a success?

I remembered working on the town as if it were yesterday. It was back in the days when Robin and I were still close, before everything changed between us. Building the huts with only Robin and a few friends from boyhood had taken a long while. A really stupid idea at the time, nothing like it had been done before. The Secret Woods belonged to no one, simply an expanse of forestry that fell under Etheland's boarders.

At first it was just a childish fantasy, a game we played as children. Since I was the oldest, I was the one to inherit our father's territory. Thus, Robin wanted to govern a land of his own. Together, we made plans to build a town in the Secret Woods as a sanctuary for the homeless, a place where people could merely go and call home. Robin was to lead it, of course. I was to help.

Robin was able to charm people to come join the new town. It didn't take much prodding, though it was difficult at first for the people to accept a teenager as their leader. He taught those who came how to hunt and he gave them a place to stay, as well as protection. I didn't know all the details, for the town was still fairly new before I left for good. Father and Mother didn't mind the idea that their son was making a way for himself in the world, but it took Robin farther and farther away from our family.

It was when he was so enthralled in his new town, totally ignoring the home he grew up in, that our relationship became destroyed. He was still acting like a child, despite his responsibilities.

I recalled the nasty things we said to each other when he was gone for nights on end. Mother was most affected by it. Father was too. When Father got sick, Robin was there less and less. And then Father died. Robin and I got into a very heated argument after that. I remembered every word of it:

"Where do you think you're going?" I had shouted after my brother.

"Back to the Secret Woods, what does it look like?" Robin responded, his voice thick.

"Now? You're going back now?" I exclaimed. *"This is a time of grieving! This is not the time to abandon us!"*

"Like I haven't endured enough of your lectures already," Robin growled. *"I am not a child, Will."*

"Then stop acting like one! Come back home. We shall discuss this later."

"That is not my home," he stated bluntly.

"What do you mean it's not your home?" My rage boiled over. *"Get back here, now!"*

"How dare you act like Father!" Robin accused.

"How dare I? How dare you!" I spat. *"Your inconsiderate journeys are what have ruined it all! Who was it who tended to Father while he was sick? Who watched him die, waiting for a son who never gave him the time of day? Who comforted Mother, and will comfort her now, when her own son has left her? It wasn't you, Robin! It was never you!"*

"I wasn't there because there are some people who actually depend on me!" Robin shot back. *"The people back in the Woods need me!"*

"If they need you so much, why do you come back?"

"I thought I knew." He glared at me with such a passion in his eyes. *"I guess I was wrong."*

And then he'd left. The coward simply left, abandoning all of his past behind him, all of his troubles shed off of his shoulders for me to bear. I had to watch our mother die alone. I had to bury her alone. I had to grow up, run the territory, and go through every difficulty alone.

I remembered once when we were only boys and Robin and I had promised each other that we'd always be there for the other. A child's promise of forever. A brother's pledge of constant.

But Robin never came back.

"Here you go," Robin said as he returned my bow and arrows to me.

I turned to the group behind me. "What shall I shoot?"

One boy spoke up, "See that apple in that tree?"

I looked to where he was pointing. In the forest in front of me, a couple yards away, was an apple tree. All the apples appeared to have been picked, except one. Way up high it dangled, all bright and shiny red. How ironic. I nodded as I set an arrow. Raising my bow, I shot. The apple was suddenly gone and on the ground, the arrow straight through the middle.

I heard a small gasp behind me. I turned back to the kids, trying to hold back a laugh, "Next?"

One of the boys ran into the woods for a minute, then came back panting. "There's a target, way back there. Can you hit the center?"

I narrowed my eyes to find the target. I spotted it quite a ways away amongst the trees. It would only just match my bow's range. Raising my bow, I drew the arrow back, aimed and quickly released the arrow. No one saw if it hit it or not, so one of the kids ran into the woods to fetch it. When he came back all of the kids look dumbfounded, except Abby, who grinned from ear to ear.

"Told you she could do it," she taunted the other kids.

The arrow landed square in the center.

"Not bad," Robin said though he was clearly awed.

"Alright, so she can shoot an arrow, but that isn't all a knight has to do. What about sword fighting?" a boy challenged.

"Yeah, sword fight!" the kids agreed in chorus.

"Well, there is one problem with sword fighting," I responded. "It involves more than one person."

"I'll do it," Robin's voice said behind me. "I'll go against you. That is, only if you want too?"

I looked at him as I said, "It's a deal." I took a step closer to him. "But you'd better be prepared for defeat."

Robin smirked. "Don't expect me to go too easy on you."

I smiled. "I wouldn't expect anything less."

I continued to search the town for Sam. I came up to one lady and asked her if she knew where Sam was at. She shook her head. Thanking her, I started to turn away when a little girl came up to me and tugged on my shirt.

"I know where the lady knight is!" she exclaimed.

"Where?" I asked.

"Come on, I'll show you." She took my hand and led me through the town.

The girl took me to the edge of the woods, the clashing and clanging of metal against metal ringing in the air. The girl pointed with her tiny little finger. "There, that's where the lady knight is!"

I looked to where she pointed and saw Sam and Robin in an epic duel. Sam moved with grace, her skirts twirling around her ankles. Robin was smiling, of course, though the sweat on his brow gleamed bright.

"The big boys didn't believe Abby when she told them that the lady was one of the King's actual knights, so they dared her to show them what she can do. She sure did when she shot that apple and hit the target in the exact middle with her arrow! Even Robin was shocked. The boys challenged her again to a sword fight, and now she's proving them wrong again. Just look at their faces!" the little girl giggled delightfully.

I started to laugh myself when I saw all of the children, especially the boys with their mouths wide open in amazement. How long ago was it when I had the exact reaction at being bested by Sam?

I watched the two dueling swordsmen, or rather, swordsman and swords*woman*. Sam faked to the left, and Robin took the bait. She sent a blow to his sword, catching Robin off guard and sending his sword clattering to the ground. Sam pushed Robin against a tree and held her sword to his throat.

"She's won! The lady knight has won!" shouted the little girl, still clutching my hand.

All of the children cheered and whooped! Sam took the sword away from Robin's throat. He rubbed the spot where the blade had been and looked at Sam. "Good job, Sam. What I wouldn't give to have you join my own troops."

"I appreciate the offer, but I couldn't accept." Sam sheathed her sword. Turning my way, she smiled and took a step towards me before the crowd of children swarmed around her.

Robin dusted off his tunic, his eyes meeting my gaze. My gut tightened. Acting as if nothing were wrong, he strutted over to the children, beckoning them to let Sam go. They reluctantly parted for the two to walk my way. Sam's joyful smile helped me relax.

"Will!" she stated. "I was hoping you'd come soon."

Robin looked between the two of us casually. His easiness lit some frustration in my chest, but for Sam's sake, I ignored it.

"Robin was going to show us around the town," Sam went on, "if that's all right with you?"

She looked at me expectantly, cautionary emotion in her gaze. She wanted me to say yes. Sighing, I turned to Robin. A daring gleam in his eye, he raised his brow. His lack of awareness to my obvious disdain made me even angrier with him. It was as if he stared right into the face of a fearsome lion and refused to admit it's even there.

"Actually," Robin cut in, "I have some party preparations to attend to. But you two go right ahead. I'm sure Will remembers where everything is."

Before taking his leave, his eyes met mine once more and he winked. The desire to pummel him nearly took over when Sam grabbed my arm.

With a sigh, I looked back at her, finding her brow knit with concern. The anger fading away, I gave her a reassuring smile. Smiling back, Sam took my hand and led me into the village.

Chapter Twenty-One

"Don't go too fast, you might smash into someone," I laughed.

Abby giggled again as she twirled round and round to the merry music. I continued to dance with her, my feet moving to the beat, our laughter echoing throughout the village party. It's all sheer fun!

Taking a peek at Will, I caught him grinning and clapping to the music. I smiled at him and turned back to Abby who danced her little heart out. She shot her big, bright smile at me, closing her eyes and spinning around and around. I did the same, eyes closed, skirts flowing around my ankles as I let the music take over. My bare feet took rhythmic steps around the dancing area.

Old and happy memories flooded through my head. It felt just like this. Dancing round and round with Mother, Father, and even little Hanna, who could only wave her pudgy arms around. Suddenly, the music stopped and I opened my eyes. I looked around and grinned at a beaming Abby. The villagers who were watching applauded, laughing with joy.

"I think I need a break from all this crazy dancing!" I said to Abby, breathing heavily.

She nodded, needing to rest herself. She ran over to her friends as I turned to the edge of the dance area. Watching the other people laughing and dancing, I clapped my hands to the cheery tune.

"Enjoying yourself, are you?" a voice said behind me.

I turned to see Robin. "Oh yes! Very much so," I responded. "I haven't been to a party like this in a *long* time."

"I'm glad to hear it," he said. "You're a fantastic dancer."

I wasn't sure I liked the easiness in which such phrases flew from his mouth, but I responded as merrily as I could, not wanting to damage anything that could ruin the alliance, "That all depends on the type of dance and the mood I'm in."

Robin laughed, "I'll leave you to it, then. I have others I must make sure are enjoying themselves." With that he turned and left.

I watched as he walked away, soon turning back to the dance floor. The music slowly changed to a slower tune. Some of the men and women started to move together tenderly while the children left the space to watch from a distance. I swayed to the gentle tune, humming softly as I watched the couples get lost in each other's eyes. The older couples with their years of happiness and growing old together were just so sweet. And the young couples with their new love and romance reminded me of Garrick and Nancy with their new life together. I wondered where they were and how they're doing. At least they're away from the threat of war. At least they were safe. I missed them.

I almost jumped from a hand on my shoulder. Turning, I found myself staring into a pair of green eyes.

"Will," I breathed out.

"Sam," he said, holding out his hand, "may I have this dance?"

I looked down at his hand and then back up into his eyes. "Of course."

He smiled and I smiled back. I took his hand as he guided me towards the dance floor. Will stopped, turned to face me, putting his other hand around my waist as I placed my free hand on his bicep. He pulled me close and next thing I knew, we were gliding across the dirt floor. My bare feet seemed not to trip or stumble like I usually did when the Queen tried to teach me how to ballroom dance.

My eyes locked on his. I couldn't pull them away even if I wanted to, and strangely, I didn't. I looked into his eyes and saw a whole other world lying behind the sea of green. Something in them showed me that he understood. He understood my pain, maybe not in the same way, but with the same heart. I felt sorry that I shouted at him back at the castle. I knew that he knew I was sorry, even as I didn't say it aloud. Something opened in my heart though I didn't know what exactly. Maybe it was because I finally didn't feel... alone. Standing before me was someone who actually understood and cared. Though it wasn't all I felt, I didn't think I was ready to recognize what the rest of this was yet. It wasn't the right time, and I just wasn't ready.

The music stopped all too quickly. Will lowered his hand away from my waist. He lingered before letting go of my hand, though. I gave him a smile before tearing my eyes away from his.

I watched as Sam entered the hut. She looked back at me before closing the door behind her. I let out a breath I didn't know I was holding.

"Hey, big brother," I heard Robin say behind me.

"Hello," I grunted, not turning to him.

He walked in front of me, smiling. "So, what is this I see before my very eyes?"

I didn't answer him.

"Is this the very brother who had promised himself he would never fall in love because it would hold him back? If I remember correctly, your exact words were '*I will never fall in love because girls just dance around wearing fancy dresses instead of doing something important or outgoing*'. Yes, yes I believe those were your exact words," he chuckled. "And here you are!"

"Who says I am falling in love?" I asked.

"Oh come on! Isn't it obvious? I am your *brother*! I know these things even if I haven't seen you in seven years," Robin laughed.

"Sam is different," I muttered.

"So you don't deny what I say?"

"She's different," I breathed out again.

"Yes, I know. She is not like most girls. She is, after all, a knight. Sam the Lion Heart, no less!"

"No, she's much more."

"I thought so. One girl believes she is a princess. She could be for all I know!"

I laughed to myself. He had no idea.

"Well, I'll see you in the morning. We'd better start preparing sooner rather than later. This war will come faster than you'll think," he said before departing.

I didn't respond, too focused on my thoughts. Was I really falling in love with Sam? I knew I felt something while we were dancing. Like some kind of an understanding; I felt a longing, a desire—something like that.

Chapter Twenty-Two

I awoke before Sam. She lay on the only bed in the room, having finally relented when I insisted she have it last night. I could make out her face even from the other side of the room. She was so peaceful. How could anyone be so peaceful?

That new feeling returned as a kind of pressure in my chest, a pleasant aching in my core. I knew that it must be that I was in love with her. I realized it sometime in the middle of the night. After a fitful and antsy few hours of confusion and the unevenness of the ground, I admitted to myself that it must be true. I was in love with Sam, and I didn't know what to do about it.

The trampling of hooves in the distance caught my ear. If I weren't already awake, I wouldn't have heard them. Getting up, I carefully left the hut so as not to wake Sam. Walking quietly down the path through town, I spotted the newcomer quickly. He just tethered his horse, a jittery behavior about his actions.

I took a closer look, shocked to find him to be Levi. I started to approach him, wondering as to why he came. He spied me and quickly scampered my way. The look on his face said that he'd been riding quickly, gray streaks of hair framing his hollow cheeks. Once I caught up to him, he placed a scroll in my hands and said, "The King says it is urgent."

I looked down at the scroll in my hands, the royal seal glistening in the early morning light. When I raised my head, Levi was gone. Opening the scroll, I read it over and then read it a second time, just to make sure I read it right. Looking up from the parchment, I felt a new fear twist in my gut. I needed to tell Sam. I needed to tell her now!

"What is it?" I questioned, rising from bed.

"A message, from the King," Will answered.

I looked down at the scroll in my hands. "When did you get it?"

"Just now," he responded.

"Is it bad news? You wouldn't have been so urgent it if it wasn't."

He looked at his feet. "Yes, it's very bad news."

I set the scroll aside. "Tell me."

He sat in the chair across from me. "King Richard has received word that Akelin is on the move. They are preparing for battle—sooner than expected."

"How soon?"

"They'll reach the forest near the castle by next week."

My shoulders slumped. "We must prepare the men here. Quickly."

"There's more." Will looked into my eyes, as if uncertain to give me the news. "Edrick, he's escaped."

My eyes widened as an empty pit formed in my stomach. "That's impossible! How?"

"One of the servants was a traitor. She helped him."

I stood up. "This calls for extreme urgency. We must find Robin immediately! We need to discuss our plan of action."

"My men are the best archers in the kingdom!" Robin announced proudly. "Of course, with the addition of you and Will. I've seen with my own eyes what you can do and it's striking! And Will has had a lot of talent with the bow and arrow since he was little."

"Then this gives me an idea," Sam stated, her hands flying to different areas of the map on the table. "Since neither Edrick nor Akelin know about the new alliance, we'll use that against them. Your men will wait in the trees around the forest, here, fully armed. They'll wait until Akelin's army approaches from roughly here. That's when we will attack. The King's men will fight from the ground, coming from this angle, whilst Sir Hugh's men will attack from here, and your men will fight from the trees. They'll fire arrows at Akelin's men. This is our advantage."

Robin rubbed his chin and smiled. "I like it. Sneak attack; that is what you want? I like it."

"Are your men ready for a war?" I asked.

He turned to me and raised his arms. "My men are ready for *anything*!"

"I'd like to see that for myself if you don't mind," Sam stated.

"As you wish," Robin agreed.

"Let's get to work," I said. "Send a message to the King. We are to go to war."

Before we continued to discuss plans, Sam met my eyes as if conveying a message. Without averting her gaze, she asked, "Robin, would you give your brother and me a moment, please?"

"Of course," he nodded, exiting the hut.

A minute passed without a sound. What would Sam want to talk about in private? My heart pounded, waiting for her to speak.

Taking a deep breath, she started, "Will, we should go back."

Her statement caught me off guard. "What?"

"We should go back, inform the King," she continued, "help him figure this out."

"But," I tried to figure out the right words, "we can't just leave. We need to oversee Robin's preparations, make sure things are running properly."

"We have a duty to the King to be there with him in this dire time."

"We have a duty to the King to be *here* in this dire time," I insisted.

Sam didn't respond. Her shoulders drooped wearily, shadows deepening under her eyes. For the first time, I noticed how tired she looked. Strong, yes, but so tired. An urge to move to her side and comfort her gripped my chest, but I stayed put.

"Edrick has escaped," Sam's voice was soft, weakened. "Akelin has rampaged through towns all over Etheland. He burned your house and the Golden Rose. He's killed nineteen innocent people that we know of, not including the thousands of lives lost and tortured in his reign. The King has to endure all of this terror again…" her voice trailed off, her fingers tracing the ring about her neck. "I should be there with him."

Hate and sorrow filled my abdomen. I knew the truth in her words, the reasons for her wish to return to the castle. But as she had previously stated, neither Edrick nor Akelin knew of our meeting with Robin. They didn't know we were here. If Sam returned to the castle, then it would be more likely that Edrick could come back for her. Here, she was safe. There…

I shivered. Edrick escaped because of traitors inside the castle. Who was to say there were not more traitors listening, waiting for the moment to strike? The kerchief burned in my pocket, the evidence of someone spying on me when I first arrived at the castle. No, we could not go back.

Besides this, I did not think it wise to leave Robin alone. Someone needed to stay and oversee that things went according to plan. But the King needed to know of our plans.

"We cannot leave, Sam," I tried to convey my meaning in my tone. "We'll send Levi back with the plans. But if things are going as fast as we expect, we cannot leave so close to battle. We need to head out as soon as we can to intercept Akelin's men. In order to do that, we must stay."

Another minute went by as I watched Sam ponder my words. I did not dare say more. This was a decision Sam must come to on her own.

With a nod, she finalized, "So be it."

It had been two days. Two days of preparation. Two days since Levi had come with the terrible and chilling news. Two days of nonstop training, nonstop planning, nonstop worry, yet still, I had no satisfaction it's enough. We had no idea how many warriors Akelin has, no clue if we had any chance at defeating him. But after those two days and finally receiving formal agreement from the King, we headed out.

The amount of supplies we brought with us wasn't one that I felt was enough. Arrows; that's basically everything that Robin thought we needed. Of course, bows were included as were swords and other forms of weaponry to which I couldn't exactly name, for such a name had not been given to arms such as these—many designed by Robin's men.

To be perfectly honest, I was surprised to find that women had joined in on the expanse of troops heading for battle. Pleasantly surprised, for I was a female warrior, but surprised none the less. Then again, it was Robin's woods.

The amount of people was astounding. Apparently, Robin's leadership went over much more than just one little town. A whole web of towns and villages seemed to be scattered throughout the Secret Woods, so much so that the forest could be considered its own kingdom. Except Robin admitted already that he would never consider himself a king, nor his territory a country of its own. Will also seemed shocked to find out that the province expanded to such as it was now.

We set out this morning, bound for the place we expected to intercept Akelin's troops. It's incredible how soft and silent an armada could travel through the woodlands. It made it easier, I supposed, to distinguish the sound of an intruder and the sound of an ally. Though, thus far, we'd come across no such intruders. That didn't stop my sense of dread that constantly rose in my throat.

My dreams had gotten even worse lately. Akelin's face was seared into my mind, though I still didn't know how I knew it was him. And now, Edrick accompanied him in their invasions on my dreams. It'd been so bad that I hardly wished to sleep at night. It's no use. Fatigue always brought sleep, and with it, the visions. Images of King Richard being slain by the hand of Akelin was one of the worst ones. Last night, I had one of Will. In both instances, the King and Will died protecting me, making it all the worse.

I promised myself never to let anyone else die for me, not ever again. I couldn't handle another occurrence like what happened to my parents. It would break me. I'd rather die than let that happen again.

A shiver coursed through my body and a tear fell from my eyelashes before I could stop it. A hand slipped into mine. I didn't have to look to know it was Will, but I did anyway. His eyes showed his concern and comfort. I smiled weakly at him and he squeezed my hand as if to let me know he was there without any need for words.

Will was the only one who knew of my nightmares. Last night—when the horrifyingly terrible one of Will and his empty, dead eyes befell me—I woke him with my cries. I remembered weeping into his shoulder as he held me. If it had been in any other instance or with any other person, I probably would've felt embarrassed upon being caught crying so much, but I needed it, the comfort and reliability. Will was there to be that little constancy that I had needed— that I still needed.

Chapter Twenty-Three

Crouching low in the underbrush, I waited silent as a mouse. I held a bow in hand with an arrow at the ready in case of intruders. A quiver slung across my back, a sword buckled at my belt. Watching the space before me, my eyes searched for any movement. I was to meet with someone from the King's army to make sure everything was in place.

A pad of footsteps and slight jangle of chainmail caught my attention. Lifting my bow, I waited for the intruder. Out of the shadows stumbled a short, bearded man bearing a sword with a wide blade. Upon seeing his face, I instantly recognized Sir Hugh. Lowering my bow, I silently stepped out of the underbrush. Before I could say anything, the knight turned toward me and jumped back startled.

"Blast it, Will!" Hugh proclaimed. "If your hood was up, you would have found yourself without a head!"

"I didn't mean to shock you," I insisted, voice hushed.

"Shock me? Ha!" He shook his head. "I knew you were there all along! Just didn't know it was you."

Smiling, I didn't contradict. "So, everything's all set, then?" I inquired.

"Aye, the scouts say Akelin's accursed army is to come out from the other end of the clearing over yonder." Hugh pointed north. "It was just as Sam predicted, eh?"

I nodded solemnly. "Just as Sam predicted."

"And where is the lass? The King's been worried sick about her."

"She's in position, waiting for me to return with affirmations."

"Good, good," he sighed, looking up at me. "Look, Will, I haven't known you very long. But I did know your mother for a brief time. She was a fine woman, and I thought you ought to know that, though I'm not the one for sentiment," he paused briefly, "she would be very proud of you, lad, very proud indeed."

A knot formed in my throat at the thought of Mother. Pushing past it, I managed, "Thank you."

A small smile formed beneath his thick beard. Then, as if realizing what just happened, Hugh coughed and sputtered, "Well, that's that, then. I have only two favors to ask of you. First one is look after Sam, will you? She's a tough lass, but over the years she's become like another daughter to me. I'd never forgive myself if something happened to her; neither would the King for that matter."

Neither would I, I thought to myself. I verbalized my consent.

"Last favor is, when you see that two-faced tyrant Edrick," Hugh growled, "kill him."

Boiling anger filled my core at the thought of Edrick. With a curt nod, I promised, "I will."

"Good lad." He clapped me on the shoulder. "Godspeed to you, Will."

"And to you, Hugh," I said in turn.

With that, I watched as the knight trumped off to rejoin the King's army. Only briefly thereafter did I sneak through the forest to meet up with Sam.

I pushed aside a branch to see the clearing better. Looking over at Will next to me, I gave a short nod. He nodded back silently, turning to give another nod at the tree next to us so as to signal that the coast was clear.

King Richard's army waited at the bottom of the hill and Robin's men waited in the trees around the clearing, exactly how we'd planned. Will and I were in a tree, keeping a look out for the enemy.

"Sam?" Will whispered.

"I'm going to kill him," I whispered back, not turning to look at him directly. "When he comes, I'm going to kill him."

"I know. I know you are," he said softly.

"I don't know why I feel this way. Maybe because of all the trouble he has caused, all the lives he's taken, but I can't help but feel it," I admitted. "I can't help but feel that this… this is personal."

"I think I know how you feel."

"What do you mean?" I turned to face him.

"When I saw you lying unconscious during the fire at the Golden Rose, I felt the same way. And that night when Edrick proved to be a traitor, I felt it again. I still do. I feel like if I was there earlier, you would have been safe. He hurt you and I will never forgive him for that."

He looked at me with a gaze that said he would do anything to protect me. Again, the nightmare came back to me, the one of Will dying for me. I knew that if he had his way, Will would most certainly give his life for me. I couldn't let that happen.

To hide my fright, I gave him a little smile and reached for his hand. He squeezed it and sent me a little smile back. Tearing my eyes from his, I looked past the branches again. We were in the same clearing where I used to live when I was a little girl. I swallowed the lump rising in my throat, determined not to let myself crumble this time. I couldn't let my body betray me or my trauma take over. There was too much at stake.

A drop landed on my cheek. I looked up and saw dark clouds gathering above. A few more drops fell from the sky, followed by a light but steady sprinkle. I turned and looked hard at the edge of the clearing. I saw a dark figure.

I fitted an arrow in my bow and turned to Will. He got the message and set an arrow in his bow, pushing aside a branch to show the men in the neighboring tree. The signal was passed through the trees until all knew that the time for battle was upon us.

Akelin's army trudged into the clearing, leaving themselves open and vulnerable. They continued on until someone shouted an order and they all stopped.

Fear entered the clearing, drifting around the trees, whispering in its chilly, ghostly voice, *"I know that you're here. I know what you want. I know where you are."* A prickle roused at the nape of my neck as its cold breath tickled my ear with this phrase. Its boney fingers reached towards me as if ready to grip my throat.

The whir of an arrow interrupted my thoughts. I turned and saw one of the men in the clearing fall to the floor. A deadly silence filled the forest until a piercing cry took its place: the cry of Akelin. His army seemed to draw their weapons in unison; the blades jagged and wicked in appearance. Another cry filled the forest, one I recognized as Robin's cry for attack. I drew and fired my arrow along with Sam. A series of arrows flew from the trees and sank into the enemy, or at least part of them.

The King's men suddenly emerged from the cover of the forest and rushed up to meet the adversaries, swords drawn. The two opposing armies crashed into each other head on. Sam and I continued to fit, draw, aim, and fire our arrows at Akelin's men. There were so many of them! More and more came out from the other end of the clearing. An arrow whizzed past me, throwing me off balance. I quickly recovered and continued to release arrows, stunned at the sudden advancement of Akelin's army.

The tree started to shake and I looked down to see a man attempting to climb the tree. He looked up and I saw the white paint on his face, indicating this to be a follower of Akelin. I aimed an arrow at him and shot. He fell without a cry, dead. I turned away and continued to shoot. Yet another enraged bellow filled the clearing as Sir Hugh and his men flooded in to join the battle.

Suddenly, Sam stopped. She glanced at me before she started to jump out of the tree. I grabbed her arm to keep her from jumping.

"What is it?" I asked.

Akelin," she answered, "I see him."

With that, she broke away from my grasp. Before I leaped after her, I wondered. How did she know it was Akelin?

With my sword drawn, I ran into the chaos. Again, I didn't know how I distinguished that the man I saw truly was Akelin, but I could feel it. He was the face from my nightmares. I thought that's how I knew.

I slashed at a man with a painted face and stabbed another with a white handprint covering his eye. I ran, slashing and stabbing Akelin's men as I went.

The rain grew heavier. My hair was already wet from the water. At least it had not grown so heavy that I couldn't see. A man with three white marks across his face lunged at me, but I dodged just in time. Whacking him with the pommel of my sword, I sent him to the ground.

A horse wheeled up on his hind legs right over me. A memory so brief flitted past my eyes of a similar incident many years ago, but I reacted differently than I had then. I dodged the wild hooves of the steed, throwing my blade into the stomach of the enemy atop it. Before the body fell or the horse reacted, I clutched my sword and dashed off.

Continuing to run, I reached the end of the battlefield just off the point where the fight met a boarder because of the rough terrain. Catching my breath, I checked my surroundings. I stood in the skeleton of my old home. My knees almost buckled and my head spun, but I forced myself to stay focused. I couldn't show weakness, especially now. I wiped blood off my brow, blood that was not my own.

"Hello, Samantha," a voice crooned behind me. I sensed Fear screeching with glee, tracing its chilling fingers down my spine.

I turned around, knowing who it was before laying eyes on him. "Akelin."

"Sam!" I shouted, not knowing where she could've gone.

Stabbing a white-faced man, I jumped back from the blade of another and gave him a blow to the back. Spotting the attacker before my comrade, I whipped around and sliced the head off of the man about to decapitate one of Robin's men—or women. The lady warrior gave me a grateful look before she disappeared into the battlefield again, her face a look of fury.

"Will, my good friend!"

I froze before turning to face the man I hated most in this world. "Edrick."

He smiled, his long hair streaming water down his shoulders. "Missed me?"

"As a matter of fact, I've wanted to introduce you to my sword for quite some time," I sneered.

He laughed, "Funny, I was going to say the same about you."

He lunged at me, but I dodged him just in time, crashing my sword against his. I attempted a blow to his head, but Edrick raised his sword to meet mine. He pushed my blade away and swiped at my leg. I jumped back, but he still cut my shin in the process. The pain wasn't great and the bleeding's minimal, which was good.

I slashed at him, causing him to stumble. My blade sent a blow to his arm, leaving him a cut, but not a deep one. Recovering from the stumble, he made a fist and punched me in the face. Tasting blood from my bleeding lip, I allowed the rain to wash it away.

"How's that leg healing up?" I asked.

"What?" He scowled quizzically.

I planted my foot on his left calf, right where I remembered the dog bite to be. Edrick cried out in pain, lashing out by butting me in the jaw with the hilt of his sword. My ears rang, but I trashed out, running my sword across his torso. With him stunned for that brief second, I crashed my sword against the hilt of his, sending it clattering to the ground. I then kicked him in the groin without a moment's hesitation. As he doubled over in pain, I caught him and held my sword up to his stomach.

"I told you once, and now I'll say it again. You will *never* have her, not as long as I'm alive," I whispered in his ear. "This is me fulfilling that promise."

I sank my sword into Edrick's stomach, the feel of his warm blood running over my hand. He cried out in anguish.

I looked at his face and into his eyes and I didn't draw my sword back until I saw the light go out. I shoved the lifeless body away and grabbed his sword from the ground, wiping it on the wet grass. I sheathed it. It's time to finish this battle, here and now.

"How do you know my name?" I questioned.

"Oh, I know much more about you than just your name," Akelin said in a smooth voice. "It's nice to finally meet you. I've been searching for you for a long time."

"How do you know me?" I asked.

"You have your mother's eyes," he went on as if I had never spoken, "and your father's hair."

"How do you know that?" I demanded.

"And a mixture of both your mother and your father's spirit," he chuckled.

"How do you know about my parents?" I demanded again.

"Really, all I get are demanding questions? Don't I get a hug from my niece?"

My head spun, trying to grasp his words. He couldn't be...

Ignoring my confusion, Akelin said, "I've been searching for the rest of my sister's family for a long time now. After all, I was looking forward to a family reunion."

"But..."

"Ever since Lillian ran away with that stable boy, I searched for her. Even after Richard took my throne, I

226

searched. Finally, I found her in a house in the woods—exactly where we are standing, actually. She refused to come with me, so I punished her and her worthless husband." He shrugged as if this was disappointing but couldn't be helped.

My throat tightened. "How *dare* you talk about my parents that way!"

Akelin ignored my statement, continuing on as if my words were as insignificant as the dirt under his fingernails, "Come to find out they had a daughter. I, of course, had no idea where that daughter was. And then, many years later, I hear about a princess, a mere peasant adopted by the King and Queen. Radiant red hair like burning hot flames. Pale blue eyes, the same shade Lillian's eyes were, the same color eyes I have."

The wind swept back his wet hair, allowing the light to reflect his pale irises as if to prove his point. Heart thudding and breath shallow, I couldn't have ever hated my own eyes more. Eyes of the devil they seemed. Shade of malice. If my eyes were his, I wished I didn't have them at all. Better blind than behold such cruel orbs.

Akelin smiled as if he could read the thoughts racing through my mind. "So here we are. The niece I have never met before and me, in the same place that your own mother was standing when I found her."

A rage burned inside me as I stared into his eyes. I saw the resemblance between my mother and this man before me, the same dark brown hair, his eyes the same pale blue. I remembered the story that my father told me when I was little, the one that had always been my favorite. The truth of it dawned on me.

"*You* did it," I hissed between clenched teeth. It was true! Every bit of it was true! "*You* were the one who set the house on fire. *You* killed my parents!"

"I admit that I most certainly did," Akelin—my uncle— said. "But we are family, Samantha. Join me. Family must stick together."

"That didn't stop *you*!" I exclaimed.

I lunged towards him, crashing my sword against his with a new fire raging inside of me. I sent blow after blow to him, only managing to hit him a couple of times, leaving cuts. He blocked my blows with mocking pleasure on his face. He drove his thrust at my face, but I raised my sword to his, thus only a scratch left on my cheek. Akelin raked his blade across my upper arm, the wound stinging. With a sweep of my sword, I feigned an attempt to jab his sword arm. He took the bait, his attention on the sword. In one swift drawback, I turned around him and sliced Akelin across the back, the wound not fatal but painful. He cried out, staggering back.

In that moment, I caught a glimpse of him that shocked me entirely. I saw him with fear in his eyes, a hollow face much older than I could've imagined, stress marks lining his brow, and the flame of madness alit behind his irises. The warrior, the once great and terrible king I'd heard about, was near inexistent. All I saw was a desperate, aged man with only a name that gave him power. Perhaps Akelin was not the man he had once been? And then the moment vanished.

Catching me briefly off guard, Akelin threw himself at me, bashing me against an old wall remnant. My head hit the hard surface and the world started to swim. Strong hands gripped at my throat, blocking the air from getting in my lungs. I wrestled against Akelin's grip, trying in vain to pry his fingers from my neck. In a desperate, instinctive action, my hands found the knife strapped to my belt and I quickly plunged it into Akelin's thigh. He cried out in pain, releasing me from his grip. I collapsed to the ground, gasping for air.

Through hazy eyes, I made out the scene as Akelin turned and ran off with a knife in his thigh. Stumbling to my feet and gagging uncontrollably, I raced after him around a corner to the edge of the clearing.

He disappeared behind the trees. I entered the forest after him. My vision blurring once again and thrown into another fit of coughing, I leaned against a tree to catch my breath.

When my lungs stopped burning and my sight cleared, I righted myself once more. Where did he go? I slowed and looked around, wiping the rain out of my eyes. Spying fresh blood on a tree nearby, I went to it, my fingers rubbing the sticky substance as if to make sure it was real. I followed the trail of blood a little deeper into the forest.

It stopped abruptly. Cautiously, I creeped forward, my senses pricking. Suddenly, Akelin jumped out from the underbrush, bloody dagger in hand and eyes aflame. I was ready for him as he lunged. I swiped the dagger away from his with a blow from my sword. He staggered back and I struck. My sword impaled his chest and he gave a painful gasp. I backed away, ready to let gravity take its course, but Akelin only smiled as blood dropped from his mouth. He pulled my sword from his chest, face contorted in pain and madness. As soon as he flung my blade aside and started to raise his sword, I kicked him in the middle of his chest, right where I just stabbed him.

Akelin plummeted back into a very small clearing, knocking his head against a tombstone as he hit the ground. Fear's scream filled my ears. I watched the life leak out in my uncle's cruel eyes until they appeared as glassy and soulless as he always was. The terror had ended. Akelin, the cruel King, died by his own sister's tombstone and by his own niece's hand.

An arrow whizzed right past my ear, embedding itself into the forehead of my would-be murderer. Turning sharply, I eyed my brother as he joined my side. Robin gave me a cocky smile before he buried another arrow into the breast of a charging assailant. I struck out at a flailing man bearing an axe, finishing him off with a stab in the back. Robin kicked an attacker my way, unloading three arrows into the man's stomach as the limp body fell into my arms. I dropped the dead man, glaring at my brother for the move. Tearing the arrows from the man's abdomen, I groaned as I slapped them into Robin's outstretched hand.

"Why are you so angry with me, brother?" Robin questioned as he let the arrows fly once more.

"Really? You want to talk about this now?" I exclaimed as I shoved away a crazed aggressor.

"What other time are we to discuss it?" Robin countered. "You won't talk about it anytime else."

I grunted, "You know exactly why, Robin."

He punched someone in the nose with his bow. "Care to specify?"

"You abandoned us, Robin!" I cried, decapitating a painted faced devil. "You left when we needed you most!"

"We?"

"Yes, of course *we*," I shot. "Mother died of a broken heart because of you! You left a thousand problems and you left me to pick up the pieces."

"So you're angry because I left Mother?" Robin asked, shooting an arrow in another man's eye in a heartbeat. "No one else missed me?"

"You honestly think that you could've just left and there not be anyone else hurt?"

"Well, if you missed me so much— I'm out of arrows," he cut himself off. I threw him the quiver that had been on my back, covering him as he strapped it to his own. Robin then continued, "If you missed me so much, why did you never come visit?"

"Probably the same reason," I started as I tried to fend off another opponent, "why you never came back."

"You think it was pride that kept me away?" Robin sliced open the stomach of a man three yards away with an arrow. "You're wrong, brother. It was fear. I was afraid that you hated me so much still that it would be no use to go back to you and Mother."

Finally managing to shove off my opponent, I swiped my sword across the man's chest. He fell to his knees, landing on his face.

"I'm sorry, Will," Robin called over the commotion of the battle. "I was a coward. Mother deserved better. She was lucky to have you. She was lucky to have a son to be proud of, a son that was not so weak as to run away from his troubles. You were always the better man."

I felt my hate and anger melt away, even as I spilled blood. I sighed, releasing the bitter pride and relenting to the truth, "No, I'm no better a man. I shouldn't have let my anger get in the way of our brotherhood. I waited seven years for you to be the one to give in—so stubborn am I—that I never thought to be the one to come to you. I never tried to fix things, even though I'd wished them fixed. For that I'm sorry, Robin."

He unleashed his cocky grin. "Brothers?"

I nodded, allowing myself a moment to smile at him. "Yeah, brothers."

The blast of a trumpet filled the air, followed by a cry of anguish. Every head turned to the edge of the clearing. A man with white paint on his face was blowing a trumpet feverishly. The man in front of me froze, looking at me pleadingly. He dropped his sword and put his hands up in surrender. I looked around to see the rest of Akelin's men drop their weapons and do the same, one by one. A voice rose above the trumpet, "They've surrendered!"

A cheer spread through the clearing. Akelin was dead! I looked up at the sky and let the rain fall on my face. Thank the Lord! We won!

I turned to Robin, who lowered his bow. He clapped me on the back before embracing me dramatically. I knew he was only joking with the overdone affection, but I still felt tears prick my eyes. I had my brother back.

Breaking from Robin's dramatized embrace, I turned to see King Richard in full armor. He looked regal and dangerous all at once. His face was grave and I remembered the words he spoke to me what felt like so long ago, *"Even the bravest of us loathe war."* I now knew what he meant.

As I looked around, I saw many who were spared, but I also saw blood. I saw the bodies of enemies and the bodies of allies. One such form caught my eye. The woman I'd saved earlier was on the ground, her body still, an axe protruding from her breast. My stomach tightened. I didn't even know her name, yet I felt such grief for her.

I spotted Sir Hugh across the battlefield, his face spattered in blood. He appeared incredibly frightening, his face as grave as the King's, though his was more angry than solemn. Sir Levi leaned against another soldier, his face contorted in pain. A hastily made, bloody bandage wrapped about his lower leg, the lines on his face seeming to be even deeper. But these men were alive. That's what mattered.

I scanned the crowd. Sam. Panic suddenly gripped my chest. Sam. I didn't see her. Oh no! Lord, please no! Don't let it be worse than it already was.

I looked around and start to search thoroughly. "Sam!" I shouted.

A figure trudged slowly out of the forest. By the red of her braid, I knew it was her. She held a sword in each hand, one I recognized as her own while the other was new to me. What's on the hilt was clearly recognized—the Screaming Skull of Akelin. I rushed to her.

Just seconds after I trudged back into the open glade, someone came up to me in a clatter of armor. Looking up the King, I took a deep breath and stood taller.

"Akelin is dead," the words came out almost subconsciously.

King Richard nodded, his face grim.

A pit formed in my stomach, and before he could say anything, I forced out, "Father—Your Highness... he was my uncle."

I compelled my gaze to stay on him despite the hollowness in my gut. His brow knitted, a confused frown forming about his mouth. "What?"

Taking in a shaky breath, I said again, "Akelin was my uncle." Upon no response, I found myself continuing, "His sister, Lillian... she was my mother. She ran off with my father to escape. Akelin, he..." My voice broke and my eyes fell to the remnants of my old home. Gesturing to the ruins, I managed to explain, "Akelin found my parents here thirteen years ago, and killed them by burning down the house. I was eight. I had no idea..."

My sentence was cut short as the King pulled me into his embrace, cradling my head in his hand. A sob escaped my chest as I squeezed my eyes shut and tears ran down my face. Dropping the two swords to the ground, I let myself absorb the comfort of my father's presence and love.

"What are the chances that my greatest enemy's niece should become one of the two women I most love in this world?" he articulated.

My heart skipped a beat, surprised by his words. Pushing back to hold me at arm's length, the King looked straight at me. His face held no amusement, only profound seriousness and sincerity.

"You are my daughter," he stated firmly. "Nothing, *nothing*, is going to change that."

A lump formed in my throat, making it hard to speak.

"Your Majesty!" a guttural shout sounded. Sir Hugh bounded up to us. "We need to figure out what to do with these traitors."

Giving me a last squeeze on the shoulders, the King nodded in finality and turned to Hugh. Watching him go, my knees shook and my gut tightened again with the reminder of recent events. Despite the King's words, I felt a sense of dread grip my heart.

Lost in my worries, I suddenly found myself enveloped in Will's arms. Leaning my head against his chest, I wrapped my arms around him. There was almost the same feeling as when Will comforted me after my one nightmare, except I had more shock than fright this time. And there was more...

"I killed him," I whispered. "I killed Akelin."

"I know. I knew you would." He rubbed my back in a soothing way, just as he had the other night.

"Akelin, he was my uncle," I said.

Will's hand froze. "What?"

I pulled away, looking up into his green eyes as everything came out at once, "I killed my uncle. My father was telling the truth when he told me that story when I was little. Akelin was the evil King. He was my mother's brother. He burned my home. He killed my parents!"

Will studied me as if listening to even my unspoken words, but he didn't say anything.

"What if, because he was my uncle," I started, admitting the sudden terror pounding in my chest, "what if I become like him?"

"That won't happen."

"We have the same blood."

"Having the same blood doesn't define you. Having the same blood as Akelin never stopped your mother. Who you are is what defines you, not who you're related to." He stroked my hair. "You have the heart of a lion, Sam."

The heart of a lion. I didn't feel so lionhearted right now, not with the haze of battle still hanging in the air. Not with the glade dotted with the dead, the casualties of my kin's wrath. How could I have a heart of a lion? The title seemed unbefitting. I wasn't the lionhearted one, or at least not the only one. This whole adventure, from the jousting tournament to now, it taught me who were truly the lionhearted ones… and who were the cowards. What's more, bravery wasn't in protecting myself from everything, it was in daring to trust, daring to love, daring to be me. Sometimes being brave meant letting go.

A knot formed in my throat. "Will?"

"Yes?"

"I think," I said softly, "I think I love you."

Will cupped my cheek. "I love you too."

I leaned close and kissed him on the lips. Not like the first kiss he gave me at the archery competition, but a new kiss, full of meaning and love. A kiss full of promise. I finally found someone who understood me, someone who filled the emptiness inside of me. I no longer felt alone.

Epilogue

"Why on earth would she not have told me?" King Richard cried. "Over the course of nine, almost ten years she's been my daughter and never mentioned this!"

"I don't know exactly why she didn't tell you, Your Highness," I tried to explain, feeling guilty for being the one to know first and not the King. "Perhaps she didn't want to bother you—"

"Bother me!" he proclaimed. "Of course it wouldn't bother me! She's my daughter!"

My face grew hot. "I know, Sire, I only meant—"

"I know you meant no harm in it, William." He waved it off. "I just wish she would have come to me."

I stood quiet for a moment, not quite sure what was going on in the King's head. My own mind still buzzed with the prospect of surprising Sam... if we succeeded. Honestly, I would've tried to attempt this on my own, but I figured that the King might want in on the secret. Now here I was, after explaining things as best I could, waiting for the King to either join me in my search or reject.

After a while of awkward silence, I tried to prompt a response, "Will you help?"

"Well of course I'm going to help!" King Richard's burst surprised me. Without any delay, he grasped his cloak and strode off, clasping me on the shoulder. Standing there in shock for a moment, I quickly scampered after him, my heart thudding in anticipation.

"How do you expect to find her?" I inquired.

"Haven't the slightest idea," he admitted, never breaking stride. "But I'm sure Hugh will have some plans. When are you wishing to have the surprise by?"

"I was thinking the festival," I suggested. "Robin's planning a big celebration, just the thing Sam will enjoy."

"Excellent." He grinned. "I'll make sure Levi and Veronica keep Sam busy until then. We can't have her discovering our secret too soon. Perhaps then you can finally ask for her hand; that should keep her off our scent."

Halting dead in my tracks, I gawked at the King, aghast. My face grew hot and chest tightened. "How did you know?"

He turned back briefly, a smirk on his face, eyes shining. "William, my boy, I have not seen a light in my daughter's eyes so bright as when she looks at you. Yet when I see you look at her, it brings me back to when Veronica and I..." his voice trailed off. "Ah, let's just say that your feelings do not fail in being made known."

Heart racing, I couldn't help but smile at the thought of Sam. She was going to love the surprise, that's certain. As for my proposal, well, I'll have to be patient until after the festival. One surprise at a time, or at least that was what Robin suggested. Though I felt nervous just thinking about it, I knew that this was what I wanted, and I didn't want to wait anymore.

As King Richard turned away, he added, "Also, Hugh told me about the ring."

Laughing, I shook my head at my own foolishness. Sir Hugh may have been the lord of a territory renowned for its blacksmiths and jewelers, but he wasn't one to keep things to himself. I should've known he'd tell the King.

"Come now, William!" the King called eagerly. "Let's go find this girl!"

"Nancy, it's so good to see you! How was it visiting Garrick's cousin?" I asked, managing not to shout over the celebrations. It had been almost a year since the war against Akelin, and Robin must have felt it was high time for a festival.

"Oh, it was fantastic!" Nancy replied. "Although, I'm glad we left when we did. Tension is growing in Lynnia about the new king, and despite the assurances of a prosperous reign, it's hard to think the country will last long without interference from Farthend or Tarn."

The news of the other kingdoms troubled me, but Nancy changed the subject before I could question further, "I'm just so glad you're safe! It was as we'd expected. The border was closed off for the longest time because of the war and new Lynnian king, but at least we made it."

"Yes, but I'm glad you two left before it all started," I admitted.

Garrick walked up to us and said, "Excuse me ladies, but I was wondering if I could steal Nancy away for a dance."

"Of course," I assured.

Garrick led a laughing Nancy away to the dance floor. I looked after them, unable to wipe the smile from my face. My eyes scanning the festival, I found Millie and Robin dancing together. Millie spied me, giggling as she used to when finding a dance partner she fancied. I bet it wouldn't be long before Robin swept Millie off of her feet… or before Millie swept Robin off his.

Someone spun me around and pressed his lips against mine. I playfully tried to wiggle out of Will's embrace, but he just deepened his kiss. Finally, he pulled away, though reluctantly.

"Now, Will," I scolded mockingly, catching the Queen smirking our way out of the corner of my eye. I laughed as he pulled me close to him and tugged on the ribbons in my hair.

"There's someone who wants to meet you," he informed, his eyes glittering.

"Alright, who is it?"

He smiled mischievously. "You'll see."

Will took my hand and led me through the square. I waved to Elizabeth, Ulric, Samantha, Owen, and Isabel. As Will weaved me around all of the different people, I spotted Abby. She seemed preoccupied at the moment, trying to smuggle treats from the dessert table with her friends. We passed Queen Veronica, who crossed her arms and gave me an approving smile. I heard Sir Hugh laughing heartily from somewhere; I didn't know exactly where, but I thought he was somewhere near the buffet. Sir Levi was with King Richard, leaning on a cane as the two conversed. I may have been wrong, but I thought I saw the King wink at me.

Will slowed and put my hand on his arm. I raised my eyebrow at him, knowing that he was keeping something from me. He guided me to a small group of people. My eyes fell instantly on one woman, her gray hair pinned up atop her head. Something in the back of my mind itched, trying to remember where I had seen this woman before.

"Sam, I would like to introduce you to Gladys." Will grinned widely. "Gladys, this is Sam."

Gladys gasped slightly, a few tears glistening in her eyes. "Oh, my, how you've grown! It has been such a long time, Samantha."

"Oh, yes, I suppose…" I started, racking my brain to remember. And her name, it's so familiar.

"You probably don't remember me, but I could never forget you, dear." Gladys smiled, her eyes twinkling. She looked down at the ring on my finger and complimented, "What a pretty ring."

"Thank you. It was my mother's."

"I know it was. I've seen the ring before. In fact, my daughter has a very similar ring. I'm sure you know it." Gladys winked.

Suddenly everything fell into place. Gladys' face was so different since I last saw her, but now I remembered. I couldn't help but look back and gape at Will. "How did you…?"

"Let's just say that the King and I are very determined when it comes to you." Will beamed, looking at me expectantly. "Is this a good surprise?"

"Yes!" I kissed him. "Yes, it's the best of surprises!" Turning back to the woman, tears welled up in my eyes. "Where is she?"

Gladys smiled. "Here she comes now."

A fifteen-year-old girl in a bright red dress walked up to us, Will's squire John at her arm. The girl before me was the exact image of my—our—mother. Ribbons were weaved through her dark brown hair, pale blue eyes gleaming from the festivities, eyes just like mine. After fourteen years, my sister was at last standing before me!

My voice broke with emotion, "Hanna?"

"How did you know?" Hanna asked, breaking away from her grinning escort.

I smiled at her, blinking back tears as I said through the lump welling in my throat, "May I... May I see your ring?"

She hesitated before slowly raising her hand. I held out my own so our hands were next to each other. On her finger was an identical ring to mine, except instead of an emerald, a ruby was entwined in the vines. Hanna gasped, looking up at me.

Gladys wiped away tears from her rosy cheeks. "Oh, I have waited so long for this day! I could never have believed it, how far you've come. To think, you were in the castle all along!"

"Did you tell her?" I questioned, not quite comprehending the words before they came out.

"Three years ago," she responded. "I kept my promise, waited until she was ready."

"I know I've seen you before, have we met?" Hanna asked me.

"Yes, we have," I responded, tears starting to fall down my cheeks. "I'm... I'm Sam, Hanna. I'm your sister, the one Gladys told you about." I shakily grabbed both of her hands in mine. "You look so much like Mother. I can't believe… You wouldn't believe how much I've missed you."

Hanna's chin quavered, a sob escaping her lips. "Sam?"

I nodded, my own chin quivering, a knot tightening in my throat. "I've found you."

Hanna fell into my arms, crying into my shoulder. Burying my face in her hair, I wrapped my arms tightly around her, holding my sister close as if afraid she may only be a dream. It couldn't be a dream. It was too real. My chest hurt with all the overwhelming joy flowing from it. *She's here*, my heart kept thumping. I had my sister back.

Acknowledgements

I've had such a crazy journey with this book, and I wished to say a special thank you to the many people who helped make it possible!

Thank you to everyone in my family: Mom, the first to read and edit this story even when it was in the beginning works; Dad, who has been begging me for a sequel—no promises, but we'll see; Madison, for her obsession with how "adorable" my characters are; Sydney, who read this despite a disinterest in the medieval; and Kendra, who listened to my proof reading as if I were telling her a bedtime story.

Thank you to my friends at the Journey Church who wanted a copy before I even finished the book. You guys are so encouraging!

Special thanks to Sunshine for her diligent editing, polishing, and excitement, as well as making me question every aspect of my original manuscript. Because of you, I am a better writer.

Thanks to my reading team—Amanda Ross, Hailey Lungren, Samantha Wright, Aliya Koetitz, and Madison Frie—who have given me pointers and excellent critiques that have definitely helped in the final refining of this story.

And of course, thank you to my Lord Jesus Christ, without whom none of this would have been possible.

Emory R. Frie is the award-winning author of debut novel, *Heart of a Lion*, and the Realms Series. She is currently attending Berry College to further pursue her writing craft, adding explorations in playwriting and experimental poetry to her passion. When she isn't writing, Emory enjoys watching musicals, sewing costumes, reading everything she can get her hands on, and going on adventures with her friends and family. She is captivated with wanderlust and dreams of learning to fly. Raised in Oregon, she now lives in Georgia with her family and rambunctious Scottie pup.

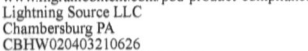